THE DEVIL YOU KNOW

A WITCHBANE NOVEL #6

MORGAN BRICE

THE DEVIL YOU KNOW
WITCHBANE BOOK #6

By Morgan Brice

ebook ISBN: 978-1-64795-023-1
Print ISBN: 978-1-64795-024-8

Cover art by Lou Harper.
Darkwind Press is an imprint of DreamSpinner Communications, LLC

1

SETH

We just might die tonight, and it won't even be monsters that kill us.

Seth Tanner hunched low over the handlebars of his black Hayabusa motorcycle and urged the roaring engine to eke out a bit more speed.

Behind him, his partner Evan Malone wrapped his arms tight around Seth's midsection and tucked his helmet against Seth's shoulder blades.

The rev of a truck close behind them told Seth their pursuers weren't ready to give up. Then a shot fired, changing the whole game.

"Fuck," Seth muttered and wove from one side of the lane to the other, desperate to keep the goons from getting a clear shot.

The gunman fired a second time and a third. Seth's luck wasn't going to last forever, and then one of the bullets would hit Evan, the bike, or him. Seth had a good idea who had hired the hitmen, and he doubted they showed up on a dark Ohio road just to send a warning.

A light ahead drew Seth's attention, and he skidded into the gravel lot of a cinder block roadhouse. Neon beer signs cast a crimson glow that attracted a row of pickups and Harleys. Red paint on white walls proclaimed it to be *Charley's Place*.

I'll take my chances on a bar fight over being shot in the back.

The charcoal Ford truck chasing them never slowed, rumbling past the bar too fast for Seth to get a good look, and then it was gone, swallowed by the night.

He faced the motorcycle toward the road, sheltered between a beat-up green F-150 and a red Silverado with a gun rack in the back window. Seth felt sure that he and Evan would be no more welcome inside than they'd been with the guys who chased them, so when their attackers didn't return, Seth hit the gas and headed back the way they came.

His heart didn't stop pounding until he slowed at the entrance to the campground where they had parked their RV. While it wasn't late, Seth was hyper-aware of the rumble of the motorcycle's engine, not wanting to draw attention. When they pulled up in front of their site, he breathed a sigh of relief.

"Doesn't look like anyone's been here," he said to Evan as he climbed off the bike and secured it. His body still hummed with adrenaline, and Seth scanned the area for danger as Evan followed him to the RV's door.

Locks and security alarm aside, the fifth-wheeler and black pickup that towed it were also protected by magical wardings, courtesy of friends with supernatural abilities. The protections recognized Seth and Evan but were designed to keep out intruders.

Seth turned on the lights and gasped when he saw the blood on Evan's jacket and realized his boyfriend was leaning heavily against the wall.

"You're hit." Seth helped Evan to sit at the table and went to fetch their medic kit.

"I didn't feel it at first," Evan said, wincing as Seth gentled him out of his leather jacket. In the light, the rip on the sleeve on his right bicep showed just how close they'd been to disaster.

"Looks like one of the bullets grazed you," Seth said, worry clear in his voice. Once he had Evan's shirt off, he could see the angry gash.

"Hurts like a mofo now," Evan replied. "I don't want to imagine what it's like to actually get shot."

"Let's hope you never find out." Seth leaned in, pressing a kiss to

Evan's lips. "Cleaning this isn't going to be fun, but I've got to make sure there aren't fibers left in the wound. I don't think it'll need stitches, or a trip to the E.R. Once I have it cleaned and treated, I'll get you something for the pain."

Hospitals had to report gunshot injuries, and that could lead to uncomfortable questions. Seth and Evan needed to fly under the radar to keep the witches they pursued and the cops off their tail.

Three years ago, a dark coven killed Seth's younger brother Jesse as part of a century-old cycle of ritual murders. No one had believed what Seth had seen that night. Then his parents died in a car wreck under unusual circumstances, and their home burned in a suspicious fire. All Seth had left was the fifth-wheeler and truck his parents intended to take on a retirement adventure and the Hayabusa he'd bought as soon as he returned from his last tour of duty.

Seth vowed vengeance, learning everything he could about the supernatural from his mentors, Milo and Toby. He went to Richmond, Virginia, to hunt down the first of the coven's witches and stop him from killing his next victim—Evan. Seth never expected to fall in love with the man he came to save. Evan made the split-second decision to go with Seth on his quest to stop the other coven members, and after almost a year together, they were headed to Cleveland, on the trail of the fifth witch.

Except that after dispatching four of the coven, Seth and Evan had lost the element of surprise.

Seth feared that Willis Osborn, the fifth witch, knew they were coming for him—and had decided to stop them first.

"Do you think it was Osborn?" Evan gritted his teeth against the pain as Seth cleaned his wound.

"Either Osborn wanted to send us a message, or we had the bad luck to run into a couple of armed assholes who shot at us for being gay," Seth replied. "I don't like either option."

"How would Osborn know where to find us?" Evan hissed as Seth covered the graze with antibiotic ointment and closed it with a butterfly bandage.

"He's a witch. I imagine there are locator spells since he knows who he's looking for," Seth said, carefully binding Evan's arm. "With the wardings on the camper and the truck, it might be harder to tell where we are. I never thought to ward the motorcycle."

"I guess sooner or later, the remaining witches would have heard about the ones we dispatched," Evan replied.

"We wondered whether they kept track of each other. I guess now we know," Seth muttered.

Seth cleaned up and put away the medic bag. When he returned, he had a glass of water and held out two ibuprofen and an antibiotic capsule, which Evan accepted gratefully.

"Rest," Seth told him, slipping his fingers through Evan's dark chestnut hair and down his cheek. Evan leaned into the touch and kissed Seth's palm.

"You got us away from them," Evan said quietly. "I thought we were gonna die."

"Not tonight. And not any time soon," Seth replied, hoping it was a promise he could keep. Evan got up to head for the bedroom, and Seth turned to the door.

"Where are you going?" Evan asked.

"I'm going to see if there's a way to ward the damn bike." Seth paused. "Don't worry. I'll be in soon."

"I'll keep the bed warm for you," Evan promised.

Seth felt too jittery to sleep, and he figured that he'd just keep Evan awake. He shouldered into his jacket, slipped his gun into the waistband of his jeans, and took a small burlap bag tied shut with red string from a drawer near the door.

It's my fault they found us tonight. I didn't ward the bike. I nearly got Evan killed because I was sloppy.

He paused on the top step to look out over the quiet campground. They had laid down protections around the truck and RV, good enough to keep out most creatures and low-level witches. It probably wouldn't protect them if Osborn decided to show up in person, but Seth doubted the witch would consider them worth his attention.

Not when he could delegate their murder to his minions.

Seth opened the leather saddlebag on the left side of the bike and stuffed the small burlap packet inside. Then he pulled a paint pen from his pocket and marked warding symbols on the inside of the bag's flap. He repeated the glyphs on the inside of the engine cover and beneath both fenders.

A root woman in Charleston had shown Seth and Evan how to make hex bags for protection and defense. She'd also made more powerful bags for them herself, and explained how to use a few basic Hoodoo rituals to deflect attention and ward off evil.

Evan and I aren't in this alone anymore. We've got friends. Allies. We've learned so much. Maybe we'll get lucky and live through this.

Milo and Toby were hunters who had taken Seth in when he was raw and angry, nearly suicidal in his grief and rage. He'd spent almost two years with them, learning everything they could teach him about the supernatural, magic, monsters, and lore. The army trained Seth in modern weapons, but Milo and Toby taught him to use machetes and blessed swords, rituals, and rote spells. Even so, Seth had been at a serious disadvantage against the first of the coven he'd fought, and while he had saved Evan, escaping with their lives and destroying the first warlock had been a near thing.

Seth let out a deep breath he hadn't realized he'd been holding when he finished warding the bike. He brushed his hand over the specially made guardian bell that hung from the lowest part of the frame, a gift from Milo and Toby, and wondered if it had helped to keep them safe tonight.

Tempting as it was to slip into bed beside Evan's warm body, he was too antsy. Seth sat down on the steps to the fifth-wheeler and pulled out his phone.

"Hey, Seth," Milo greeted him. "Everything okay?" His mentors seemed to sense when Seth needed them.

"We're outside Cleveland. A truck chased us on the bike and the passenger shot at us. One of the bullets grazed Evan."

"Fuck," Milo growled, and Seth heard Toby in the background, insisting that the call be put on speakerphone.

"You two all right?" Toby asked, his gruff tone covering concern.

"Evan will be okay. I got him patched up, and he didn't need stitches," Seth replied. "It could have been a lot worse. I think Osborn knows we're coming for him."

"They were going to figure it out sooner or later," Milo replied.

"Even if the coven members don't like each other, they'd be stupid not to keep tabs just for self-defense. Hard to miss when four of them die off in the same year."

"I put new wards on the bike to help it deflect attention," Seth replied. "And I'm giving credit to the demon bell for getting us home safe tonight."

Legend held that small bells with protective images and sigils kept "road demons" from harming the motorcycle's rider. The one Seth's mentors had gifted him was likely far more authentic than those offered in the average biker shop.

"Watch your step," Milo warned. "If Osborn considers you a threat —even a minor one—he'll try to get rid of the 'distraction.' He likely knows what happened to the other witches who didn't take you seriously."

"We're ahead of the game this time," Seth assured him. "We have better intel, thanks to Simon and Travis, so we know the current iden- tity of the disciple, and we're pretty sure we know where his anchor is hidden. When we were in Charleston, Rowan taught us more rote spells, and Mrs. Teller showed us some Hoodoo we can use. We've got new sigils and relics and weapons, thanks to Cassidy's friends. That's a big advantage."

Their allies were psychics, mediums, former supernatural special ops agents, witches, and conjure women, bound together by friendship and a mutual commitment to protect the world from paranormal threats.

"You could hand the whole thing off, you know," Toby said. "Let someone else take it from here. Plenty of other hunters out there who wouldn't be tempting fate by being a descendant."

Seth knew his mentors worried about him and Evan. He'd thought about passing the baton to someone with stronger magic than the minor ability he and Evan possessed, someone who could fight the witch disciples head on and overpower them.

"None of those folks noticed a century of murders or stepped in to make it stop," Seth said after a pause. "And besides—do you really think the other disciples wouldn't come after us, even if we did quit? We'd be looking over our shoulders for the rest of our lives."

He took a deep breath, trying not to snap at the older men, reminding himself that they were seasoned hunters themselves. "I get it—there's a lot of evil out there. But the disciples made this my fight when they killed my brother and tried to kill Evan. It's *our* families they've preyed on for one hundred years. It's personal."

"Which can be a good reason to give it to someone else," Milo replied. "It's possible to be too close to something. Clouds your judgment."

Seth tried not to let his temper flare, knowing that the two men were worried about his safety. "Now that we've got allies, I promise to ask for help when we need it."

"Travis and Brent aren't too far away in Pittsburgh," Toby reminded him. "And Mark Wojcik says he's got someone he trusts in Cleveland who might be helpful. I'll get the information and pass it on. Don't be too proud to make use of them."

"I promise I'll call if we need backup. And I don't think wanting to see this through is pride—more like responsibility. My ancestor helped start this when they hanged Gremory. I intend to end it."

One hundred years ago, a sheriff's posse hanged a dark witch named Rhyfel Gremory near Seth's hometown of Brazil, Indiana. Gremory had cursed the lawman and his deputies and called down the vengeance of his witch disciples to hunt and destroy his killers.

Gremory's death magic conveyed near-immortality on his twelve apprentices, who each chose one of the deputies' families to be unwitting participants in blood magic and betrayal. Instead of trying to save Gremory from the noose, the disciples turned on their dying master and worked a spell to bind his spirit. Every twelve years one of the witch disciples would kill the eldest of his chosen family. During the ritual murder, the disciple used the victim's life energy in a protection spell to keep Gremory's spirit contained while they further drained his magic to give themselves a power boost.

Seth and Evan were both descendants of those doomed deputies, the eldest of their generation in the direct descendants.

But the witch disciple made a serious mistake in Seth's case. He'd grabbed Jesse instead of Seth. And by doing so, he'd created an enemy who swore to wipe out all of the coven's warlocks.

Seth hadn't waited to go after the disciples one year at a time. He and Evan had destroyed four in the past twelve months, forcing the witches on the defensive and weakening their hold over Gremory's trapped spirit. The disciples sped up their sacrifices even though they gave up some of the power gained by doing so, afraid they might lose their intended victims or that Gremory's spirit might break their spell.

Along the way, Seth and Evan had learned more minor magics, spells, and curses, gotten better at tracking witches, and surviving arcane battles. They'd also made friends with people who used their own supernatural abilities to stop dangerous creatures. That had kept them alive this far, and Seth hoped with all his heart it would be enough to get them both safely across the finish line.

"We're here whenever you need us," Toby affirmed. "How's Evan?"

Seth sighed. "Rattled. Can't blame him. I'm a bit of a mess too. Planning to order a Kevlar jacket for Evan."

"Not a bad idea," Milo said.

"I wasn't worried about bullets," Seth replied, shaking his head at his blind spot. "I figured any attacks would be magical."

"There might be a bright side to all this," Toby said. "If Osborn sent the shooter, he sees you as a threat or an annoyance—but not enough of one to send witches or handle you himself. Probably figures that the other disciples you killed were sloppy and made mistakes. He's cocky. You can still surprise him."

"I don't mind being underestimated," Seth replied, with a smile that showed his teeth. "I can work with that."

He ended the call and promised his mentors that he and Evan would be as careful as possible and stay in touch.

Seth stared into the darkened campground. The windows in some of the other campers glowed, not a surprise considering it was relatively early in the evening. He wondered if their temporary neighbors were retired, vacationing, or running from something of their own.

When did it get this complicated? he wondered. *I didn't know anything about witches, and I didn't believe in magic or monsters. No one else picked up on the pattern of deaths in all those years. But I can't un-know something after I've learned it. And if I don't stop the murders, who will?*

Seth heard a sound inside and got up immediately, worried about Evan. He went in and locked the door behind him and set the alarm, activating the wards. For a second, he debated whether to leave his gun in the kitchen but decided he felt safer with it close at hand.

He hung up his jacket, toed out of his boots, and turned off the lights as he made his way to the bedroom, putting the gun in the night-stand drawer. "Evan?" he called quietly, unwilling to wake his partner but wanting to provide comfort.

Evan didn't respond. Seth closed the distance, watching for the rise and fall of his lover's chest by the dim glow of the bathroom light. Evan twitched and flinched, deep in sleep but restless. *Nightmare*, Seth guessed.

He stripped out of his clothing and cleaned up quickly for bed. Then he pulled on a pair of sleep pants and a T-shirt and slid beneath the covers next to Evan.

Evan turned toward him, half-awake, and nestled close. Seth held his breath, not wanting to keep Evan from the rest he needed to heal.

"I can't sleep," Evan murmured. "Every time I drift off, the night-mares start."

Seth pulled him close and carded his fingers through Evan's soft hair.

They fit together perfectly. Both men were six-foot-three, but Seth was dark blond with brown eyes, while Evan had chestnut hair and hazel eyes. Seth pressed a kiss to Evan's temple. "I'm here. You're safe."

"I know." Evan wriggled impossibly closer. "Talk to me."

Seth chuckled. "What do you want me to say?"

"Tell me about 'before.' Jesse. Your family. You never say much, and I want to know."

Evan's request caught Seth unprepared. "Really?"

Evan nodded against Seth's shoulder. "Please."

Seth was quiet for a moment. Memories were never far from his mind, but talking made it all the more real.

"My folks weren't perfect, and neither was our family, but most of the time, we got along," Seth recalled in a quiet voice. "Jesse and I had

9

our spats. Brothers do. But we were the only ones allowed to pick on each other. If anyone else tried, we closed ranks fast."

He sighed. "We drove our parents crazy. We weren't out to make trouble; we just had our own ideas about how to have fun. We raced dirt bikes. Made a kamikaze zip line in the forest that was a lot of fun until I broke my arm. Played hide-and-seek in a salvage yard and got chased by junkyard dogs. I'm amazed Mom wasn't completely gray by the time she was forty," he said with a chuckle.

"Sounds like more fun than I had."

"Maybe that's also why I don't say much—I know it was different for you." The quiet darkness had a confessional feel, making it easier to say difficult things. They lay beside each other, shoulders touching, both staring at the ceiling.

"We're not talking about me. I want to hear more," Evan said.

"Jesse was a big nerd. He loved comic books, superheroes, horror movies, and stories about space," Seth recalled fondly. "He got me into those, and I dragged him with me to action flicks and paintball games and concerts."

"When did you tell him that you were gay?"

Seth's lips twitched in a sad smile. "He knew before I ever said anything. To tell you the truth, I think he knew I was gay before I realized it. Jesse saw my first relationship implode, even if he didn't know that's what it was, and he tried to talk me out of going into the Army to run away. Second biggest mistake I ever made."

Seth knew that Evan didn't need him to explain. The biggest mistake he'd ever made was agreeing to go camp out with Jesse at a "hell gate" tunnel to shoot a spoof video and have an excuse to hang out and drink beer. Something had knocked Seth out, and when he woke, Jesse was gone. He found Jesse's body on the other side of the tunnel, bloody and savaged.

"Happy memories. Go on," Evan prompted.

"Mom liked to bake, but she didn't get much time to do it except at holidays. She'd join these crazy cookie exchanges where all the women in the neighborhood would make their best sweets, and then everyone got a variety. We had to freeze some because we couldn't eat them fast enough," Seth said.

"How about your dad?"

"My grandfather wasn't around much when Dad was little, so he swore he'd do things differently. If we were in a science fair or a play or a BMX race, Dad was there. He and Mom were looking forward to visiting as many national parks as they could with the RV when they retired, but everything went wrong just a few months before they got the chance," Seth told him.

"Back to Jesse," Evan said. "What did he want to do?"

"He liked programming and engineering. Jesse was always taking things apart to see how they worked and building cool stuff from odd parts," Seth said.

"I wish I could have met him. I know you miss him."

"Every day." Seth turned to Evan. "Your turn. It's only fair."

Evan let out a long breath. "I have two younger brothers. Jim, by two years, and Parker by four. Growing up, Parker and I were inseparable. Jim and I were close enough in age that I think he felt he had to compete with me. Mom and Dad fed that, but I never did."

"I was the black sheep, so I think Jim and Parker felt they had to make up for me, but for different reasons," Evan said. "Jim was embarrassed because I wasn't into sports or hunting or chasing girls. Even before I was outed, there were rumors. Jim never wanted any 'gay-by-association' to rub off on him." His tone turned sad and bitter.

"And Parker?" Seth nudged, not wanting his boyfriend to get stuck in a bad place.

"Parker was usually my accomplice. He tried to cover for me, did his best to convince people I wasn't as gay as they thought." Evan sighed. "He meant well, tried to protect me, but—"

Seth knew the key points of Evan's story, even if his boyfriend hadn't shared every detail. His first teenage "real" boyfriend had been guilted into making a public confession of their "sin" at a youth camp, outing Evan in the process. Evan overheard his parents' plan to send him for conversion therapy or he'd be kicked out. He'd left before they had a chance. Evan got by on bartending and waiting tables, couch surfing during tough times.

"Have you heard from them?"

Evan was quiet long enough that Seth wasn't sure he'd reply.

"From my parents and Jim? No. I didn't change my number—they just don't call. I don't want to argue, and I'm not going to 'change my mind,' so we'd just be retreading old ground. What's the point?"

Seth heard the sadness in Evan's voice. He knew his boyfriend had accepted the reality of the situation, but he'd never stopped hoping, deep down, that things could be different.

"Parker found ways to contact me after I left that they couldn't trace. He'd email me from school or call me from his friends' cell phones. We talked every month or so. I knew he wanted me to come home, but he didn't ask."

"Would you have gone?"

Evan hesitated, then shook his head. "I couldn't. It would have been suicide of the soul. Parker knew that. He didn't ask it of me."

"It's been a while since you left. Do you still hear from him?"

Evan looked sad. "Not as often, or as regularly. We never went more than a few months without connecting until you and I went on the run. It hasn't been as often since then. I didn't tell him what we were doing, of course. I've kept everything vague for his safety. Even if he doesn't know the whole truth, keeping secrets put some distance between us."

Seth reached out and took Evan's hand. "I'm glad we found each other. If I'd stayed in Indiana and you'd never left Oklahoma, we might never have met."

There was no way to balance their losses, but if that trauma had put them in a place where their paths crossed, then something good had come out of the worst days of Seth's life.

Evan squeezed Seth's hand. "I think about that too. I'm glad we found each other, although I'd never have wished what we lived through on anyone."

"I love you," Seth said, feeling like he was whispering a secret to the moon that shone brightly through the RV's window.

"Love you too," Evan returned as exhaustion slurred his words. "But now—gotta sleep."

Only a few minutes later, Seth heard the deep, regular breaths that let him know that his boyfriend was asleep, but Seth remained staring at the ceiling, adrift in memories, for a long time.

2

EVAN

A FEW DAYS MADE A BIG DIFFERENCE. EVAN'S WOUND HEALED QUICKLY, and he did his best to remind Seth that they didn't dare sit still for too long or Osborn would find them, distraction spells notwithstanding.

"I just don't want to go into this with you off your game," Seth grumbled as they rehashed the same argument.

"Neither do I. But I feel much better. And we need to get moving before Osborn closes in on us," Evan pointed out.

He patiently allowed Seth's daily wound check and treatment. Evan knew the worst was behind them and that they couldn't use the injury forever as a reason to take it slow.

Seth's phone rang. He glanced at the caller ID. "Hi, Teag! What intel do you have for me?" He changed to speakerphone mid-sentence.

"—our theory that the witch disciples were each other's enemies was wrong—or at least, flawed," Teag Logan said. Teag's magic made him an expert hacker, and his research was always excellent.

"From what I've found, your Cleveland guy, Osborn, teamed up tight with the St. Louis witch disciple for several twelve-year cycles. They were brothers. I'm not sure what the venture was—considering what we've seen elsewhere, probably some trafficking scheme involving people with paranormal abilities."

Teag paused. "Something happened—I'm not sure what—and when the dust settled, Osborn was still standing, and the St. Louis witch was dead. On the bright side, that means you have one less witch disciple to hunt."

"We appreciate the information. Any chance you might be able to dig up details about what Osborn and the St. Louis witch were doing? It might matter," Seth said.

"I can try. The good stuff is hidden, but that just makes it a challenge," Teag said, and Evan could hear the grin in his voice.

"Did you find out anything more about the victim who's next in line?" Evan asked.

"Derek Nelson is a twenty-nine-year-old officer with the Cleveland Metropolitan Police. He's a legacy—Nelsons have been in the CMPD for more than a hundred years," Teag reported. "He's the oldest of three—one of his siblings works for the National Park Service, and the other is in college. His father was the witch disciple's victim six years ago. So by the way the timing went until now, Derek would have six witch-free years left—"

"—before he ends up gutted on an altar," Seth finished the sentence.

"The reports we turned up blamed some kind of large, feral dog for the father's death," Evan mused. "At least, that's what the articles online said."

"That's the line that got spread to the public," Teag answered. "When I hacked the CMPD system, I found emails questioning the nature of the attack and wondering if it might not have been a human hiding his work by adopting the 'style' of an animal killing."

"Close, but not quite," Seth muttered.

"Derek's won plenty of commendations for his work," Teag noted. "Unofficially, I get the impression he's a stubborn hard-ass with some anger management issues who took his dad's death really hard. The first year afterward, he was written up for getting into some fights off-duty."

"Dirty cop?" Seth asked.

"I haven't found anything to suggest that," Teag replied. "More the opposite—a little too 'by the books.' Married young and divorced—no kids. From the little I could find online, he's not very social. Spends his time with a few close friends playing video games and hiking. That's not much to go on, except to give you a head's up for when you meet him," Teag warned. "It's not likely to go well."

"Thank you. The research helps a lot," Evan added. Having help lightened the burden because arcane lore was never easy to find or quick to search. Overlooking details, no matter how small, could be deadly.

"Any time. Take care—and be careful," Teag warned.

Evan ended the call and looked at Seth. "Comments?"

Seth shrugged. "I won't object to having one less witch disciple to fight. I'm honestly surprised that only two of them were working together. They could make more money by teaming up, but they'd have to be able to trust each other."

"What did you make of Teag's intel on Derek Nelson?" Evan asked.

"I think he sounds like a pain in the ass who is going to give us second thoughts about saving him," Seth replied, grimacing. "The real question is—has he put the pieces together to realize someone is killing the oldest of each generation in his family, or do we have to start from scratch and explain it?"

"Aside from the hard time I gave you, the other intended victims had an inkling that something wasn't right and that they were in the crosshairs," Evan mused. "And I can tell you that the way my folks recounted family history, they must have seen the pattern but didn't want to acknowledge it. No one ever sat me down to tell me that I was next in line to be horribly killed. I would definitely remember." He sighed. "Then again, maybe they didn't think that was a bad thing."

"Hey," Seth said gently. "Don't go there. What's past is past."

Evan snorted. "This whole crazy quest to kill the witch disciples is all about how the past isn't over. The witch disciples are killing people about a century-old grudge. And the victims' families are deceiving themselves about the pattern because they don't want to see what's in plain sight. We'd have a much easier time if we didn't have to start the discussion by convincing Derek that ghosts are real."

"You've got a point." Seth's lips twitched with fond amusement.

Evan shifted in his chair, and Seth leaned against the wall. "Still want to go exploring tomorrow?"

Seth nodded. "That's what we came here for. Do you feel up to a hike to the old observatory? Maybe we can get a sense of whether Osborn's anchor is still there."

"Sounds like a plan," Evan confirmed.

AFTER BREAKFAST THE NEXT MORNING, EVAN AND SETH SET OUT FOR THE site of the old Warner and Swasey Observatory, a Cleveland landmark that had gained more notoriety as a beautiful ruin after its decline than it had achieved when it was in working order.

"This place is amazing. I can't believe they'd shut down something like this and just let it rot." Evan could hear the wonder in Seth's voice as the remains of the observatory came into view.

"What good is an observatory if there's so much light pollution that you can't see the stars?" Evan replied. "That sealed its fate."

"Still..." Seth eyed the old building, and wonder colored his tone. A low, rambling brick building stretched across the top of the knoll. In the middle atop a boxy center section sat the retractable dome that had once housed a large telescope that made several groundbreaking discoveries in its time.

Now, plates from the dome were missing, exposing the rib-like understructure. The telescope had long ago been relocated, as well as the astronomical library. The building sat abandoned, although investors had toyed with ideas for its re-purposing over the years.

"Why would Osborn leave his anchor hidden in a piece of land that he doesn't own?" Evan voiced a question that had been bothering him since Seth had discovered the anchor's possible resting place.

Every witch disciple had an anchor, a receptacle of stored power that both strengthened them and also bound them to a place. The anchor and the amulet—a spelled talisman the disciples usually wore around their necks—plus the ritual sacrifice of a direct descendant from one of the deputies' families opened a rift that let the disciple draw power from the trapped spirit of their old master, Rhyfel Gremory—and kept Gremory trapped by blood magic.

Destroy the anchor and amulet and prevent the ritual murder, and Gremory could turn on his disciple and destroy him.

"Osborn's been in Cleveland since the witch disciples scattered after Gremory's death in 1900," Seth replied, leading them closer to the ruin. "Plenty of time to establish a new identity and create a role with the observatory after it opened. If Osborn became one of the trustees of the observatory, he probably figured he could keep an eye on something hidden in plain sight."

"There's plenty of magical lore about the position of the stars," Evan mused.

Seth nodded. "Exactly. Then Osborn had to drop out of sight for a while, so no one caught on that he never dies, and by the time he came back, the place was abandoned. But as long as it doesn't get sold, there's no hurry to move the anchor. Not a bad plan."

They made a careful inspection around the outside of the building before picking a padlock to let themselves inside.

Evan's nose twitched at the combination of mold and dust that hung heavy in the musty air. The lobby's fancy terrazzo floor, once barely recognizable beneath the dirt and plaster dust, celebrated the signs of the zodiac. Some explorer before them had cleaned away the grime to reveal the magnificent pattern beneath.

While the brick and stone exterior endured the elements largely unscathed except for a shroud of ivy and the damage to the fragile dome, the inside had not fared as well. Peeling paint and disintegrating plaster marred the walls. Water damage brought down portions of the ceiling. Despite being boarded up, the wreckage of the seats in the theater was ample proof that animals had invaded.

"Such a waste," Evan murmured.

"I agree." Seth sounded distracted. "Help me find the sundial on the floor. It looks like a fancy manhole cover. It's copper turned that funny shade of green. Travis and Teag both agreed it was the most likely place to hide the amulet."

Light filtered in through filthy windows as they moved carefully through ruined hallways. Bits of plaster crunched beneath their boots, and roaches skittered when their flashlights illuminated the shadows.

The farther into the old observatory they went, the more Evan's intuition told him to get the hell out. "Do you feel that?" he asked Seth.

Seth nodded. "I think it's an aversion spell. There's less vandalism and tagging in this area—did you notice? Maybe the warding to keep the anchor safe makes people not want to go near it. I think the hex bags help us be able to keep going."

Evan's hand went reflexively to the pocket of his coat where he had protective bags, as well as salt, aconite, and iron filings. *At least there aren't stories about the observatory being haunted. A dark witch is bad enough.*

"In here." Seth gestured to the amphitheater where students and the general public once beheld planetarium shows. He pointed at a copper embossed seal inset into the floor of the theater's lobby, green with verdigris and darkened with grime.

Despite the defense of the hex bags and their protective medallions, Evan's skin crawled. "How do we break it open?"

Seth took several photos of the seal with his phone. "I'll send these to our friends and see if anyone can read the markings. I'm sure Osborn didn't leave it here without serious wards."

"Let's go," Evan urged, fidgeting. "We got what we came for."

Seth nodded, looking just as uneasy. "Yeah, I think you're right."

They headed back the way they came.

Two strangers blocked the doorway. "That's far enough," the taller man said.

With one twitch of his fingers, the shorter man sent Seth flying backward to crash into a pile of rubble. Before Evan could react, he was also airborne, landing hard on the filthy floor.

They hadn't brought guns, and their hidden knives were no help against witches. Evan tasted blood in his mouth from a split lip and felt a warm trickle start from his hairline. A glance assured him that Seth was moving, but neither of them would last long if their attackers dished out more of the same.

Seth's right hand shot forward, and a streak of fire streamed from his open palm, igniting the trash around the feet of the two witches.

The strangers had to break off their attack to stamp out the flames or risk catching their clothing on fire.

Evan saw his opening, and tossed a handful of pebbled plaster into the air, then spoke a word of intention and accelerated the pieces toward their attackers to hit much harder than he could have thrown them, like a spray of buckshot.

The witches yelped, and this time, Evan sent the torrent of fire, aiming between the two witches to catch both their down jackets. Seth sent a volley of plaster chunks from the floor—larger this time, pelting their attackers as the two men were forced to stop, drop, and roll.

Evan knew their limited abilities were no match for true witches, but their unconventional use of small magics might throw attackers off their game enough to provide an advantage.

"Run," Seth murmured. The air in the lobby smelled of burned feathers and melted nylon from the witches' down jackets.

They bolted outside, leaving the door ajar behind them, and ran to the truck. Both of them were covered in dust and dirt from the filthy observatory floor.

Evan shook his head like a dog, trying to dislodge chunks of plaster and strands of cobwebs from his hair. He jumped into the passenger side and buckled up just as a police car came around the corner with its lights and siren on.

This can't be good.

"Fuck," Seth muttered, as he slid behind the wheel.

Evan knew that trying to get away would just make them fugitives before their quest in Cleveland had even begun. Seth gripped the steering wheel tightly while Evan tried to recall all the compromising items stored in the bed toolbox.

The patrol car pulled up behind them, lights flashing. Both men sat still, hands visible in their laps, as the cop sauntered up to the driver's side window. "License and registration," he snapped, warily eyeing Seth and Evan. His name tag read *D. Nelson.*

"Hello, officer. Can we help you?" Seth sounded cool and collected. Evan's heart was in his throat, and he hoped he didn't need to answer the cop.

"Got a report someone broke into the observatory. Right after we had a tip that two guys in a black truck with out-of-state plates were trouble," the cop told them. "Give me your license and registration—or we can handle this down at the station."

"Are we being arrested? If so, on what charge?" Seth kept his voice neutral. "My lawyer will want to know." He handed over the paperwork and gave a bland smile.

Evan knew the cop's bluster was bogus. They were sitting in a legally parked truck with nothing to connect them to the observatory. He wondered who put the cop up to confronting them and whether Osborn had anything to do with it.

The cop—Nelson—glanced over the two items and handed them back, more proof to Evan's mind that the whole effort was harassment since he didn't have the dispatcher run the information.

"Are we free to go?" Seth's smile turned brittle.

"Cleveland isn't the place to stir up trouble," Nelson warned. "We'll be keeping an eye on you."

Seth pulled away from the curb and was careful to drive at the speed limit until Nelson and the observatory were out of view.

"Want to bet that whoever sicced the witches on us also called the police?" Seth asked when they had put some distance between them and the cop.

"I thought about that. For all his magic, Osborn must be nervous if he's making an effort to get rid of us before we even make a move," Evan replied.

"Notice anything about the cop?"

Evan shook his head. "Besides being an asshole? Not really."

"The name tag read *D. Nelson*. Want to bet that was Derek Nelson—next in line to be Osborn's victim?"

"Shit. Pretty ironic if he gets sacrificed because we're cooling our heels in jail after he arrested us," Evan replied.

"Let's hope not."

Evan looked to Seth. "Seriously—how do we save the guy if he's already convinced we're out-of-town ruffians?"

Seth shrugged. "I've got no friggin' clue. We've never had the witch disciple be this far ahead of us before. I get the feeling we're going to

have to be quick, or we'll end up facing a lot more cops and witches—
and it won't go well."

Evan stared out the windshield for a while as they drove back to
the fifth-wheeler. Finally, he broke the silence.

"Before I met you, I knew our family had a 'run of bad luck' with
men in each generation dying too young. Sometimes they disappeared.
In other cases, the mangled bodies got blamed on different causes. Car
accident. Farm machinery mishap. Factory tragedy. I could accept that
we were 'unlucky,' but the idea that magic was involved? Too much to
believe," Evan said ruefully. "Maybe Nelson's the same way."

"Except you knew you needed help to stay safe," Seth pointed out.
"Nelson's a cop, from a family of cops if our intel is right. I have a
feeling that he's not going to want to admit that he needs anyone, even
if he's in over his head."

"If Nelson—or his anonymous informant—convinced the police
that we're troublemakers, it could get hard to maneuver," Evan
warned.

"Short of just walking up to Osborn and blowing him away, stopping the ritual takes time," Seth remarked as he set out plates and
utensils while Evan filled water glasses.

"I can't imagine that would go well, no matter how stealthy you
tried to be about it," Evan said drolly.

"No kidding. But the issue is catching Osborn when he's got his
intended victim, and he's started the ritual." Seth pointed out. "Technically, Nelson should be safe for a couple more years. We screwed up
everything by taking the disciples on faster than the cycle."

"Jumping the gun has worked so far," Evan replied. "If he's so
nervous about us being in town, maybe Osborn isn't as powerful as we
thought. With nearly half the disciples dead and the rituals happening
more often, Gremory's power boost isn't doing as much for him or
lasting as long."

"I hadn't thought about that—but you're right. Losing the other
witch disciples and their rituals—and doing the sacrifices with less
than a year between them weakened Gremory, so he can't supply the
same recharge. It's more dangerous too, because the regular sacrifices

aren't going to be enough to keep Gremory contained—and if he gets free, there'll be hell to pay," Seth said.

"We don't have to test that theory," Evan cautioned. "Osborn might still be plenty powerful without getting a signal boost from the other witches. If you recall, we've nearly died a few times."

"I try not to think about that."

Usually when they first rolled into a town looking for a witch disciple, Seth and Evan would make a point of eating at a different "local's joint" each night to pick up interesting gossip. But after the run-in with Nelson, they stopped for take-out from a local diner and brought it back to the RV, figuring it was best to keep a low profile.

Evan had ordered chicken fried steak with mashed potatoes and green beans, while Seth got a burger and fries. Since the diner had a tall case of tempting desserts next to the register, Seth added a piece of cherry pie for himself and a slice of chocolate cake for Evan.

When every meal might be your last, Evan found it difficult to order a salad. Training and then running for his life tended to provide plenty of exercise.

After dinner, Seth poured them each a couple of fingers of whiskey, enough to take the edge off.

Seth's phone rang, and Evan recognized Teag's ring tone. "You'd better get that," he said.

His boyfriend sighed. "I know. But it's going to harsh my mellow."

"I'll mellow you," Evan promised, and he knew Seth could read the heat in his gaze.

"I'll hold you to that." Seth answered the call. "Hi, Teag. What have you got for us? Let me put you on speaker."

"Hi, Seth. Hi, Evan. I've hit pay dirt out on the Darke Web when I looked up info on Osborn." Teag's hacking surpassed even Seth's exceptional skills. The Darke Web used ensorcelled encryption and was the favored online resource of supernatural creatures and those with paranormal abilities.

"What did you find?" Seth asked.

"So…the witch disciple currently known as Osborn was an apothecary back in the day," Teag replied. "As he reinvented himself over the last hundred years, he stayed in pharmaceuticals. Then he branched out into illicit drugs for the supernatural community."

"Like what?" Seth asked, surprised.

"Strength enhancers, hallucinogens that work on non-human metabolisms, roofies that make it easier to erase memories and immobilize victims, pills that will give a buzz to an immortal, or let them sleep without dreaming. He's supplying a cartel, and there are links to another trafficking ring that was uncovered several months ago," Teag told them. "It's pretty ugly. The legitimate packs and nests are not on Osborn's side, but they don't dare oppose him head-on."

"Fuck," Evan muttered. They knew about the online trafficking groups that had been exposed within the supernatural community for seizing young shifters or people with psychic gifts and selling them into servitude or for shifters to big game hunters with "exotic" tastes. Their friends had helped to take down some of the trafficking kingpins, but the problem was widespread and not easily contained.

"So we're not just going up against Osborn," Seth clarified. "He's going to rally his customers, who stand to lose a major supplier if we stop him."

"That's what it looks like," Teag admitted. "It might be a good time to call for backup. Mark Wojcik gave me a name—Joe Mack. He thought Joe could help you and provide some protection."

Seth fidgeted, and Evan could guess what his partner was thinking. *He's weighing the value of bringing in reinforcements versus trusting a stranger.*

"All right," Seth replied. "Go ahead and text us Joe's contact info, and please let him know we might be in touch. I want to get my feet under me before we throw in a wild card."

They'd worked with others many times, including Teag. But always before, they'd known those allies from trading information online, even if they hadn't met in person. Evan understood Seth's reluctance to bring in a total stranger, even one who'd been amply vouched for.

"Will do. Stay safe," Teag cautioned. "And keep your eyes open—Osborn is definitely connected."

Seth ended the call and sighed. "We should probably call his contact."

Evan could hear the reluctance in his boyfriend's voice. "It's not a bad idea to have someone who not only knows the city but the local supernatural community. That doesn't mean he gets to tell us how to do our job."

Seth grimaced. "It's just hard to trust someone I don't know to have our backs."

"I trust Teag and Mark. That's a pretty strong endorsement," Evan noted.

"Yeah, yeah. Okay. How about tomorrow, after we go to the main library downtown?" Seth replied. "They have old maps that haven't all been digitized, and I want to see if I can narrow down possibilities for the location where Osborn's been doing his rituals."

"Sounds like a plan," Evan said. "I want to look at the old photos and public records. We have holes in what we know about Osborn's 'reinventions' over the years. Filling in the gaps might not matter—or we might find something important. But it's worth a few hours to see what they've got."

"We can go in the morning and be back by early afternoon. That gives us the rest of the day to run down any leads we find." Seth stretched, arching his back and twisting his neck from side to side, working out the kinks that came with spending too much time driving.

"I can help with that," Evan offered, dropping his voice to let Seth know he meant more than a massage.

"Oh, yeah?" Seth raised an eyebrow with a glint in his eyes.

"Rumor has it I have 'good hands,'" Evan said with a smirk, repeating something Seth had told him a few days before when Evan jerked him off.

"Hmm. That's tempting." Seth pretended to consider the idea.

"Happy ending guaranteed," Evan added.

"Sounds good to me." Seth stood and stretched again before he held out his hand and led Evan back to the bedroom.

The king bed took up most of the space, but for an RV, the room was generously sized. The bathroom was not, especially for two grown men, so shower sex was out of the question.

"Take off your shirt and lie down." Evan stood back to enjoy the show as Seth stripped off his Henley and the T-shirt beneath it. Seth's toned chest and strong arms had Evan chubbing up before they'd even gotten started. The bulge in Seth's boxer-briefs when he dropped his jeans made it clear the feeling was mutual.

"Like what you see?" Seth teased.

"You know I do."

Seth stretched out face-down as Evan took off his shirt and jeans and reached for massage oil in the nightstand drawer. He double-checked to make sure he hadn't grabbed the lube by mistake—doing that once was enough. Then he straddled Seth's hips and warmed the oil between his palms before leaning forward and kneading tight shoulder muscles.

Seth's pornographic moan ensured that Evan's cock was rock hard. He paused to adjust himself and ground against the thin material covering his lover's ass. There was no way Seth wouldn't notice Evan's hard-on, and a wiggle of his hips assured Evan that his message had been received.

Evan worked down from the tendons in Seth's neck, giving special attention to knots he found. They had learned a lot about massage from trial and error, and Evan had watched a few online videos to pick up more pointers.

"Yeah. Right...there." Evan's thumbs dug into a tender spot. Evan varied the pressure and the type of stroke, concentrating his effort where the muscle felt rock hard. "That's it. Don't stop."

Evan continued to work his way from Seth's broad shoulders down each arm, then rubbed and kneaded the muscles of his back to the V of his waist. The warm oil let his hands glide over Seth's skin, soothing tension.

"Feeling more relaxed?" he teased, knowing that Seth was nearly boneless between the warmth and his touch.

"Umm," Seth hummed. "You know what would make me even more relaxed?"

"Coming your brains out?"

"You must be a mind-reader."

Evan tugged at Seth's briefs and quickly shed his own. This time when he straddled Seth's ass, his stiff cock fit perfectly between well-muscled ass cheeks. That created a pleasant friction for Evan as he massaged Seth's lower back and teased a happy ending.

"I'm all for a different kind of rubbing." Seth's voice was a low rumble that heated Evan up from inside.

"How do you want it?" One of the many things Evan appreciated about their relationship was that both were comfortable switching.

In reply, Seth rolled over without bucking Evan off. He reached out to let his fingers trail down Evan's face. "Want it like this, want to watch you ride me, want to see your eyes when you come."

Evan's cock was already hard and leaking, and Seth's proposition just made him ache all the more. Seth handed him the lube. "Open yourself up. I want to watch."

Evan squeezed lube into his palm and slicked his fingers. He reached behind himself and slid one finger into his tight hole, angling his body to make sure Seth had a view of that digit slipping into his ass. Seth's breath caught; his pupils were wide and dark, and his lips were slightly parted.

"So beautiful," Seth murmured.

Evan added a second finger, letting his head fall back as he worked himself open. Seth splayed his hand over Evan's heart, then rolled first one tawny nipple and then the other between his fingertips. Evan rocked backward and forward before inserting a third.

He looked at Seth's flushed face, took in the arousal in his eyes and his stiff prick standing at attention. Without ever losing eye contact, Seth took the lube and slicked his cock.

"Ready to ride?"

Evan shifted forward, kneeling with Seth's dick poised at his hole. Then he sank down, taking his lover's cock balls deep.

Hearing Seth's pleasured groan was worth the burn. Evan rose, then lowered himself again, starting a rhythm. Seth reached out and grasped his hips, meeting Evan's thrusts with his own.

Evan swiveled his hips, moving in a figure-eight the way he knew Seth liked, not just for how it felt, but because he loved the sinuous way Evan moved. Seth's fingers dug into his skin, hard enough to leave marks. Evan loved to see the evidence the next day, just like he relished a sore ass as a reminder of a thorough fucking.

They moved faster, matching each other's movements. Evan's heart thundered in his ears, and he felt his climax begin as heat low in his belly. Seth's eyes never left his, but his breath came short and fast, and a sheen of sweat beaded on his forehead.

"Come for me, Evan," Seth growled. "Now."

Evan knew Seth was close. He could feel him trembling, feel the sharp thrusts of his hips. His release seemed to rise from the base of his spine, and then it crested, and Evan cried out Seth's name as his come spilled hot over Seth's fist. Seconds later, he felt Seth come deep in his tight channel. He loved watching Seth's face as pleasure overtook him, knowing that he could wring that response from Seth's body.

When the last aftershocks subsided, Evan folded forward and kissed Seth long, slow, and dirty.

"I love you," he whispered, nipping gently at Seth's lips. "So, so much.

Seth slid his tongue across Evan's lips. "Love you too. More than anything." He rolled them over and slipped out.

"Be right back," Seth murmured, brushing his lips against Evan's. He padded to the bathroom and returned a few moments later with a warm, wet cloth, then tenderly wiped Evan clean. Seth tossed the cloth toward the bathroom, and then they slid beneath the covers.

"I'm yours, forever. You know that, right?" Seth carded his fingers through Evan's hair and pressed a kiss to his temple.

"Uh-huh," Evan replied, blissed out and rushing toward sleep. "Same here. Yours—always."

3

SETH

"Pretty impressive, just sayin'," Seth said as they wandered into the Cleveland Public Library's main branch. The original 1920s-era building had a white marble facade with pillars, and the recently remodeled interior had restored the ornate ceilings and other architectural features.

"It's a temple to knowledge." Evan's hushed voice sounded equally awed.

Seth unfolded a map of the building he had grabbed on their way in. "So there's the original building and then the new wing. This place takes up a whole city block. Unfortunately, the things we came to look at aren't close to each other."

Evan shrugged. "How do you want to do this? Stay together or split up and cover the territory faster?"

Seth hated to let Evan out of his sight. But it felt like the clock was ticking, narrowing their window to get to Osborn. "Let's split up. We can text each other every half hour. And we've got salt and hex bags in our pockets, plus it's a pretty public place for Osborn to come after us."

"Are you sure?" Evan looked worried.

"It's only for a couple of hours," Seth replied. "The sooner we can finish here, the faster we can get back to taking care of business."

"Be careful," Evan warned.

Seth glanced around, then he pulled Evan into an empty row between shelves and kissed him slow and deep. "Love you," he murmured.

"Love you too," Evan answered. "See you back here soon."

Seth headed to the map room while Evan went in search of old photographs and public records. The huge building was maze-like despite the map and plenty of directional signage. The main section of the library was busy for a weekday morning, bustling with retirees, young mothers with children, and job seekers.

Once Seth crossed into the more specialized collections, the library seemed deserted except for the reference expert behind the information desk, a woman who reminded Seth of his mother. Her name tag said *Janet.*

He stopped to explain what he was looking for and opened his messenger bag for examination. The hex bags were in the pockets of his jacket, and his obsidian knife—good for getting past metal detectors—was in a hidden compartment of his bag.

"Please use the cotton gloves to handle the maps," Janet warned as she gave him a quick tour of how and where the maps were stored and then led him over to the big oak study table.

"Pencil only—no pens allowed on the table. I recommend taking pictures if you find something relevant—but no flash photography. Just ask if you need any help—I step away occasionally, but never for long. And I love solving puzzles, so if you aren't finding what you need, just holler—quietly," she added with a smile.

Seth assured her he would and then pulled out his notebook with the list of locations he had identified from his online sleuthing. He and Teag had already identified property owned by Osborn in all his reinvented identities.

Seth wanted to find out how the sites and their surroundings had changed over the past century. He wasn't entirely sure what he was looking for, but he knew he'd recognize it when he saw it. Seth had learned that sometimes serendipity revealed what was needed if he trusted his instincts.

Two places in particular caught his eye; a defunct rehabilitation hospital and the Detroit-Superior underground trolly station built and then abandoned as time and traffic changed.

As he worked his way down the list of locations, Seth took photos and texted tidbits to Evan, saving his work to the cloud. They'd broken enough phones while battling the bad guys that Seth no longer trusted keeping anything valuable on his device.

Evan shared photos and comments of his own, keeping up a running text conversation. The small, glass-enclosed map room seemed warm, and Seth shrugged out of his coat, keeping it behind him on the chair.

He ferried maps back and forth between the table and the big wooden flat storage drawers. The deeper he dug, the more engrossed in his research he became.

"That's convenient," Seth muttered as he cross-checked an address for the old rehab hospital owned by the shell corporation that concealed Osborn's many identities.

It's right next to the Detroit-Superior station. Desolate tunnels that tourists are only allowed to visit once a year. I can't imagine a more perfect place to carry out his rituals without being disturbed.

Seth snapped a few more pictures and realized he was due to check in. Before he could text the photos to Evan, a noise drew his attention.

He looked up, on alert. Janet's deserted desk and the empty map room made the restricted area feel too isolated and exposed.

"Janet?" Seth leaned out of the map room doorway and stage-whispered to the librarian. When no one answered, he palmed the obsidian knife from his bag, grabbed the hex bags and his phone from the pocket of his jacket, and ventured toward her desk.

"Janet?"

Suddenly the library's quiet seemed sinister instead of restful. Seth's instincts went on high alert. He circled Janet's desk but didn't see any sign of trouble. Her papers were in neat stacks, the computer had gone to its sleep screen, and nothing looked amiss.

He heard a muffled noise in the stacks behind the desk. Seth thought about calling Evan, but if Janet was in trouble, he couldn't wait for backup. He gripped the knife and moved closer toward the sound.

The first row of stacks was empty. In the next row, a crumpled form lay on the floor.

"Janet!" Seth rushed forward, wondering if the librarian had passed out. He knelt beside her and checked for a pulse, relieved to feel a steady heartbeat.

He felt a sharp jab in his neck. Seth plucked out the dart and threw it away, but the damage was done. The drug hit him fast and hard, making his vision swim and his balance wobble. Seth gripped the obsidian knife, ready to make a hopeless last stand as two large goons closed on him.

Seth swung a punch and missed by a mile, staggering with the force of his swing. The guy on his left didn't miss, landing a punch to the jaw; a second blow sent him sprawling as the drug rushed through his system. The other attacker strode up and patted Seth down, relieving him of his phone, knife, and hex bags.

Seth felt an odd ripple of energy race up and down his body from head to toe. It felt hard to breathe, and his heart pounded. Pain spiked in his temples, and a trickle of blood started from his nose.

Magic. Fuck.

Someone had lured Janet away from her desk, used her for bait to draw Seth away from his locked room, and like a fool, he'd gone. Now without his hex bags for protection, he was an easy target.

The rippling energy grew stronger, buzzing across his skin. He tried to push up, and he wanted to shout for help, but his body refused to obey.

Everything seemed to happen in slow motion as Seth's muscles gave out. His face hit the floor, but he barely felt the impact. Sight, sound, and touch shut down one by one like someone had flipped switches.

Are they going after Evan next? I promised him I'd be safe. I fucked up, and now I'm not going to be able to protect him.

Everything faded, and Seth was lost in the dark.

～

"HEY, LAZY ASS! TIME TO GET UP. BREAKFAST IS GETTING COLD, AND I already ate all the bacon," a familiar voice called from outside his bedroom door.

Seth groaned and struggled to wake. He blinked, trying to clear the sleep from his eyes, and momentarily panicked, not knowing where he was. He took a few seconds to look around and get his bearings.

His room at his parents' house hadn't changed since he left for the Army six years ago. Seth wondered if his parents had kept it untouched as a good luck charm, a way to guide him safely back.

He'd been warned that going home after his tour of duty would be difficult. Slipping into what should have been familiar now felt like trying on clothing that didn't fit. Seth felt uncomfortable in his own skin, and he wondered how long it would last until he adjusted.

A pillow hit him in the face, and when Seth batted it clear, his brother Jesse leaned into his room, grinning.

"I've still got great aim," Jesse crowed. "C'mon, Army brat. Mom made *waffles*. She never makes those. Now I know I need to go to a combat zone to get a decent breakfast."

Seth wasn't prepared for the flood of emotions that washed over him. As much as he loved his parents, Jesse had been the person he'd missed the most while he was overseas. They'd video called as often as Seth's circumstances permitted, trying to keep the six years spent apart from widening into a gap that couldn't be bridged.

"Do we even own a waffle maker?" he asked, rolling out of bed.

"You're coming down to breakfast like that?" Jesse teased with a nod to the worn, comfortable sleep pants and T-shirt Seth wore. "How quickly you lose all of your military standards."

"Bite me," Seth replied, but the fond tone took the heat from his response.

"You'd give me indigestion." Jesse flipped him off. "Don't make me drag your scrawny ass downstairs."

Seth had put on twenty pounds of muscle while he was in the Army, and Jesse had filled out as well, no longer the gangly kid he'd been when Seth shipped out. "Scrawny" didn't really describe either of them.

"I'll be there in a minute," Seth said.

Jesse grinned and held up Seth's phone. "Take your time. I want to read all your messages."

"You wouldn't—"

Jesse wiggled the phone back and forth. "Want to bet?"

"Don't you dare!"

"Make me stop!"

Seth lunged from his bed, making a wild swing to take back his phone. Jesse danced out of his way, teasing him by holding the device just out of reach.

He grinned once Jesse was out of sight. They'd always been close, and the fondness he felt for his little brother hadn't faded just because they grew up and spent a few years on separate continents.

Seth took a military shower—two minutes was all he needed. He'd planned on enjoying the luxury of taking his time and not having to share a facility with the rest of his platoon but...*waffles*. It only took a few minutes longer to towel off, comb his hair, and get dressed.

"Five minutes...pretty fast for a geezer," Jesse teased when Seth came downstairs, emphasizing the two-year age difference.

"Guess they moved you up from sippy cups while I was gone," Seth joked in return. He kissed his mom on the cheek and made a plate for himself, then sat across from Jesse.

"Where's Dad?" Seth wondered why a simple question made his stomach tighten.

"He took the RV over to the dealership to upfit a couple of things," she replied. "It's going to be the Waldorf-Astoria on wheels by the time he's done."

"Like you don't spend every spare minute mapping out itineraries," Jesse replied with a sidelong look.

Seth's mom grinned, and a blush came to her cheeks. Linda Tanner was a pretty woman at sixty, and he knew from old photos that she'd been a real beauty when she and their father met. Their father had aged into what might be termed "craggily handsome," giving Seth hope for what he might expect to look like himself someday.

No one would mistake Seth and Jesse for anything but brothers. Same tall, broad-shouldered lanky build as their dad, same dishwater blond hair and brown eyes, with the thin face and high cheekbones they got from their mom. Both of them stood roughly six foot three, within a fraction of an inch of each other. Not only did the resemblance make their status as siblings unmistakable, but anyone who watched them together for more than a few minutes quickly realized they were inseparable.

Except when I ran away from a broken heart by signing up to get shot at. Not my best move.

It had taken enlistment and time in a hot zone to realize that running didn't solve anything. He'd lost six years with the people who loved him, trying to forget the one who didn't.

He vowed never to make that mistake again.

"Is this what you've been feeding Jesse while I was eating MREs?" Seth asked with a grin. "This is fantastic."

He dug into the Belgian waffle, topped with what he suspected might be homemade blackberry chutney. Fluffy scrambled eggs filled the other side of his plate, and despite Jesse's taunts, he really hadn't eaten all the bacon.

"Are you kidding? We had cold cereal and Pop-Tarts while you were gone. She's just making sure you don't re-up," Jesse said, but Seth had the sense his brother was only partly joking.

"It wasn't quite that bad," his mom protested, barely hiding a smile.

Jesse gave an exaggerated eye roll. "Maybe not. There were pancakes from time to time."

"What's on your agenda, now that you're out of uniform for good?" Linda asked Seth.

Every time he heard her voice, his throat closed and tears sprang to his eyes. *Weird. Must be part of coming home.*

"Waiting for the Hayabusa to be delivered." Seth felt a flutter of excitement thinking about the motorcycle he'd saved up to buy. "I've been looking forward to that sweet bike for a long time. Beats hell out of a Jeep."

"Don't worry—with the way Dad's been fussing over the RV and that new truck, Mom should be plenty jealous," Jesse replied with a mischievous glance at his mom. "Can a truck be someone's mistress?"

"Jesse!" Linda smacked his arm playfully.

"You know it's true. I've never looked at a girl the way he looks at that truck," Jesse protested.

Linda shook her head fondly. "We've been talking about going to see so many places, and there was always some reason we couldn't. When we first got married, we didn't have the money. Then you were both so little. When you got older, there was school and activities, and it just wouldn't work. Now here we are, retiring. We've been adding to our list of places to go for a while."

She brought her hands together like a flying bird. "Now the two of you are launched. So it's our time."

Seth grinned. "I'm so glad. You two deserve it, putting up with us."

Linda smiled. "We couldn't be prouder, and you both know it."

Seth had always known on some level that he was fortunate to have his family. Six years of hearing other people's stories about their drama had confirmed that he was one of the lucky ones. His parents loved him, and he had a brother he would die for, whom he knew would do the same.

"Let's go eat stuff you couldn't get while you were gone," Jesse said through a mouthful of waffle and bacon. "Anywhere you want to go, bro. Chinese, pizza, Mexican—whatever. See if you can still put the all-you-can-eat places out of business." He waggled his eyebrows.

"You're talking lunch while you're still eating breakfast?" Linda asked.

"And now that we're both legal, we can see how you do with all-you-can-drink," Jesse continued.

Linda elbowed Jesse. "Not when you're driving."

"Of course not," Jesse replied, with the choirboy innocence that had gotten him out of everything since they'd been kids.

The appeal of gorging himself and testing his drinking limits had faded early in his military career, but this was Jesse, looking for a way to reconnect with his big brother, and Seth couldn't say no.

Maybe it was a good thing for him that I was gone for a while. It let him come into his own without always being my "little" brother. But I'll always regret losing that time together.

"You're on," Seth said. He felt a strange urgency to grab his mom and brother and hold them close, tell them how much he loved them, and all the other things people never actually put into words.

Seth chalked it up to having been in life-or-death situations for the past few years. He'd seen men die screaming for their mothers on the battlefield, half a world away from home. There had been moments when he didn't think he'd make it back, and he thought of all the things he'd never said to the people he loved most.

"Try not to get too sick to eat dinner," Linda said, with an indulgent resignation as if she knew she'd already lost this battle. "We're ordering pizza from Niccolo's."

Seth grinned. "They're still around? Best. Pizza. Ever."

Jesse drove his second-hand Mustang, and Seth squashed his long legs into the passenger seat. "Good to have you home," Jesse said, keeping his eyes on the road. "I thought Mom was going to single-handedly cause a candle shortage burning votives for you."

"Mom is a lapsed Lutheran," Seth protested.

Jesse shrugged. "Just sayin'. She would have made a deal with the Devil himself if she thought it would bring you home safely."

"Don't say things like that," Seth said, suddenly uncomfortable on a level he couldn't explain. "That's not the kind of thing you joke about."

Jesse gave him the side-eye. "You sure you're okay? I mean, I know you saw your share of action, and I respect the hell out of you for doing what you did. But none of us are going to think less of you if you need to see a therapist. PTSD and all that shit."

They rode in silence for a while. Seth had the oddest feeling of belonging somewhere else, something he chalked up to having recently gone from a desert war zone to suburban America.

Seth cleared his throat. "I was wrong," he said, knowing he needed to speak his truth. "I'm sorry."

Jesse gave him a weird look. "What are you talking about, man?"

"Running off and enlisting just because Colin and I, um, had a falling out. That was severely stupid," Seth confessed. "I made a major life decision for all the wrong reasons. I missed out on being with you, Mom, and Dad. It wasn't until I was in my first firefight overseas that I realized Colin didn't ever mean as much to me as you guys."

Jesse returned a wobbly smile. "I knew you'd come to your senses sooner or later," he snarked, although Seth heard the break in his brother's voice. "Man, it's good to have you home."

Jesse took Seth on the food tour of all the places he'd missed during the years he was deployed. Everyone greeted Seth like a long-lost son, and he realized around the time they hit the third stop that Jesse must have talked about him a lot in his absence.

"Dude, what did you tell them about me?" Seth hissed when the servers at the fourth bar fussed over them.

Jesse shrugged. "Just that I had a highly-decorated combat vet brother who was coming home, and we needed to do him a solid."

"You what?" Seth managed, still taking in Jesse's smug grin.

"Today's all about you, bro. I missed you like fuck, you know," Jesse replied and then paused. "So...when are you going to come out to Mom and Dad?"

Seth knew he gave his brother a deer-in-the-headlights stare. "What?'

"Oh, for fuck's sake. Colin? Newsflash—you're gay. When do you intend to tell Mom and Dad? Because I promise, it won't change anything."

Seth just stared at him. "How did you know?" His heart beat faster, and he felt his palms sweat as he tried to think of how he might have given himself away.

"Seriously? I'm your brother. You had a 'falling out' with your 'best friend' Colin bad enough to make you basically join the Foreign Legion? That's not friendship—that's a broken heart. And, you think I didn't notice you not noticing the cheerleaders but being glued to the tight pants on those football players?" Jesse said, giving Seth a "duh" look.

"Whether anyone else ever picked up on it, I've always known. I was just waiting for you to find the right time to tell me, so I could say it didn't matter."

Seth reeled, taking in what Jesse said. "You're okay with it...me? I thought Mom and Dad might freak—" *Did they know about Colin too?* he wondered.

Jesse gave a rueful grin and shook his head. "I brought the subject up a few times—very sideways, I promise," he said, raising his hand to stave off protest. "Asked whether they'd have kicked either of us out if we told them we were gay."

"And?"

He shrugged. "They didn't care. I believe them, given how angry they've gotten over some of the anti-gay politicians."

"Huh." Seth didn't have any reason to think his parents wouldn't take his announcement well, but he'd planned to take things easy and get comfortable with the homecoming before tossing out any surprises. "Good to know. I promise I'll tell them. Just...not yet. Let me get settled."

"Gonna be a non-event, I'm tellin' you." Jesse shook his head fondly.

"I hope so," Seth replied. "And—thanks. For having my back...and not minding."

Jesse leaned forward and locked his gaze with Seth. "You're my brother. Nothing changes that."

Jesse's reply warmed Seth's heart. He felt a knot of anxiety untangle that he hadn't realized existed. At the same time, an odd thought crossed his mind.

I could have sworn we had this conversation before, somewhere else. Must have dreamed it. Coming home is really messing with my head.

They stopped for frozen yogurt and lingered to play vintage video games in the small arcade next door. Nostalgia washed over Seth, reminding him of all the times he and Jesse had whiled away afternoons there back in high school. Nothing had changed, which seemed true of the whole town.

"Don't forget Mom's planning on feeding us dinner," Jesse said as they left the arcade.

Seth groaned. "You took me to all my favorite places. I might never eat again."

"But it was good, right?" Jesse sounded a little nervous, and Seth wondered how long his brother had been planning to celebrate his return.

Seth couldn't hide his broad grin. "Yeah, it was *real* good. Not just the food. There's still a lot of catching up to do, but we're getting there."

"No rush," Jesse told him. "We've got plenty of time."

They walked in companionable silence for a while. Brazil, Indiana, wasn't a big place. Its claim to fame was being the birthplace of Orville Redenbacher, the popcorn king, and Jimmy Hoffa, probably the most famous missing person in America. Being a bedroom community to nearby Terre Haute brought in new residents with cash and kept the downtown vibrant.

"So..." Jesse said. "You got any plans?"

Seth looked at him. "Besides finding room for dinner?"

Jesse rolled his eyes. "I mean like getting a job. You gonna stick around here or strike out for the big city?"

Seth snorted. "You mean Terre Haute? Or Indianapolis? At least there's a big gaming convention in Indy." He shook his head. "Wasn't really planning on either one. I want to use the computer surveillance skills I learned in the Army and start my own security company. White hat hacker, stress testing systems, that sort of thing. I could work from anywhere."

"Oh yeah?" Jesse brightened. "That's a great idea. You'd be really good at that."

"How's work going?" Seth asked. "Do you miss college?"

"I like my job. It's mostly programming right now, but I think I'll be able to transfer into engineering. I loved college, and I miss it sometimes. The campus was big, and it took some getting used to, but there was always something going on. And being able to commute saved a lot of money."

Seth and Jesse had talked about his high school graduation and college applications while Seth was deployed. Indiana State was affordable, well-ranked, and close to home. When Jesse had gotten accepted, Seth couldn't have been prouder.

Brazil wasn't a tourist town, so the people they passed on the sidewalk were likely to be locals. The weather was mild considering it was nearly Halloween, and Seth figured that he and Jesse weren't the only ones trying to enjoy a walk before the cold settled in to stay.

Seth noticed a dark-haired man walking half a block ahead of them. He couldn't see a face, but something about the way the man moved made Seth certain they knew each other. Before he could think too much about it, he and Jesse had to stop for a traffic light, and when they could cross, the other man was gone.

"Something wrong?" Jesse asked.

Seth shook his head, although the déjà vu feeling remained. "No. I just thought I saw someone I knew...but I didn't stay in touch with anyone from high school, and I imagine a lot of people have moved on. So I can't figure out who it might have been."

"It's a small town—if someone lives here, you'll see them again," Jesse assured him. "C'mon—we can't be late for dinner."

When they walked back into the house, Seth paused, drinking in the familiar sight. He had dreamed about coming home so often while he was overseas, and it was hard to convince himself that he was really back.

"Dinner's on the way—go wash up and set the table," Linda called to them. "Your dad will be here soon."

Bustling around the kitchen felt so familiar that Seth could almost forget that years had elapsed and that he'd ever left. They laughed and joked as they nearly bumped into each other more than once, and by the time their father arrived, everything was ready.

"This smells fantastic," Brian Tanner said as he walked in carrying a pizza with the works from Niccolo's.

Seth decided that retirement looked good on his dad. His parents owned a local construction and remodeling company, and while its success provided well for their family over the years, Seth knew the stress took a toll. The recent sale seemed to take a weight off both parents' shoulders.

"How did the fifth-wheeler upgrades go?" Seth asked, intrigued and amused by his dad's sudden obsession with going on the road in style.

"All finished. We are going to have the classiest home on wheels on the highway."

Seeing his dad's wide smile was worth the price of the camper. "Did you know that there are RV clubs? You join and people go on trips like a caravan or meet at the campground. Even if you don't make new friends, at least the other campers might not be total strangers."

"Like a motorcycle gang, but with trailers?" Jesse teased.

Brian grinned. "Exactly! Maybe we should get matching jackets."

"I am not wearing a Hell's Angel vest," Linda called from the dining room.

Brian slipped up behind her and kissed her ear, winning a surprised squeak in return. "You'd look good as a biker chick."

She gave a playful swat at his hand on her shoulder, but the pleased smile made it clear she was flattered. "Does that make you a leather daddy?"

Jesse choked, and Seth barely hid a snicker. He wasn't sure his father got the joke, but from the wicked gleam in his mom's eyes, he knew Linda meant what she said.

"Looks like you're going to have a very interesting retirement," Seth said, barely managing to keep a straight face.

The pizza was as good as it smelled.

Seth's mom talked about the locations she wanted to visit, while his dad described all about the fancy improvements to make a comfortable camper luxurious.

Seth told funny stories from his deployment. Much of the work had been grim and dangerous, but he and his friends still managed to have some good times, and Seth didn't want to forget the happier moments.

He loved the insights into Jesse's college life that his brother's tales provided. Seth knew he'd missed some big moments in Jesse's life, and hearing the stories helped fill in the empty spaces.

When they finally left the table, Brian couldn't hold back a yawn. They had started late and lingered over conversation, and it was nearly ten by the time Seth and Jesse carried the dishes to the sink.

"You two crazy kids go on and get some rest," Seth said to his parents as he ran water into the sink. "We'll clean up."

"Don't overload the dishwasher," Linda warned.

"They're adults. They can figure it out," Brian told her, tugging her toward the hallway. "See you in the morning."

Seth watched them go, unsure whether to be amused or disturbed by his parents flirting on their way to their bedroom.

"Is that...new?" he asked, feeling like a failed chaperone.

"I chalk it up to midlife madness," Jesse replied. "I mean, it's good they're happy together, right? They were probably getting it on all the time we were younger, but they weren't quite so open about it. Not that there's anything wrong—aw, fuck. They're still our parents and it's weird."

"As long as I don't walk in on them," Seth murmured. "That would be—"

"Awkward." Jessie and Seth spoke at the same time and started laughing far too hard for what the situation warranted. Maybe it was the wine from dinner, but Seth thought it was yet another phase of homecoming—feeling giddy with relief to be safe and reunited.

"Want to watch a movie?" Seth asked.

"I was thinking about poker, actually," Jesse said. "Figured you might have learned a few tricks in the Army, and I've played some with my friends at school. You owe me a rematch."

"Seriously? Dude, that was six years ago."

"You won sole use of the car for a whole week," Jesse replied. "And you were a dick about agreeing to drive me anywhere."

"I really was, wasn't I?" Seth smirked.

"Paybacks are hell," Jesse warned.

"Big talk, little brother. Put your cards where your mouth is."

"You're going down."

Best two-out-of-three games later, Jesse won fair and square. They played for who had to wash dishes for a week since Jesse had his own car now, and Seth's motorcycle would give him his own wheels.

"Who did you go to college with—card sharks?" Seth complained good-naturedly. "I thought soldiers were supposed to have an edge when it came to cards and gambling."

"One of my friends—Tony—earned his tuition money playing in poker tournaments," Jesse said off-handedly.

"Now, you tell me?" Seth wasn't annoyed—he was intrigued and would have loved to have met the friend.

"And one of my other friends is a math whiz. He's a card-counter—been banned from the casinos in Indiana, so he has to go out of state when he needs to raise quick cash."

Seth gave Jesse a look. "Do Mom and Dad know that they sent you to college to consort with gamblers and people with loose morals?" he asked with an exaggerated, arch tone and waggling eyebrows.

"They sent me to college. It's synonymous."

Once they put the cards away, it was close to midnight, but neither of them had an early morning, and Seth had a lot of movie-watching to catch up on.

He and Jesse had always seen the new superhero movies and blockbusters together, ever since Seth had gotten his license at sixteen. They smuggled cheap candy in the pockets of their cargo pants, splurged on a refillable bucket of popcorn big enough to share, and bought supersize drinks, making it a real outing.

Missing the big-name movie releases had been hard for Seth, and he'd been unprepared for the ache of loneliness it brought when he was half a world away.

"I bought the DVDs for all the big movies that came out while you were gone," Jesse said, taking the puffed-up popcorn bag out of the microwave. "Figured we could watch them when you came home." He opened a cabinet door. "I stocked up on gummy worms, Reese's Pieces, and M&Ms."

Looks like Jesse and I were on the same wavelength, even so.

"Thanks." Seth hoped his voice didn't break with emotion. "I've been looking forward to seeing all the movies I missed with you."

They settled on the couch with the popcorn and the candy between them. Seth cracked open two longnecks and handed one to Jesse. With the lights out and the new, larger screen TV his folks bought while he was gone, the experience wasn't as different from the theater as Seth had feared.

They picked a movie at random. The opening credits seemed to go on forever.

"So...got a girlfriend?" Seth asked as they watched the screen.

"Haven't had time," Jesse replied. The darkness made conversations confessional, creating an ease for discussing sensitive topics. "Engineering deserves its rap for giving you no social life, so no one from college. There's a girl at work I want to ask out; she's on one of my teams, but there's never been a good opportunity."

"Sounds promising."

Even in the dark, Seth knew Jesse's gaze slid to him. "How about you? Now that you're out of the Army and there's no more 'don't ask, don't tell,' got anyone you're planning to look up from the old days?"

"You've got to be kidding." Seth shook his head. "I figure I'll have to go to Indy to meet someone. Not that there aren't gay men in Brazil or Terre Haute, but they're so far in the closet they can see Narnia."

"But you want to meet someone?"

"Sure. Of course," Seth replied. For some reason, the idea of going clubbing or swiping right made him feel uncomfortable, as if it would be cheating.

Can't cheat on the loser who broke my heart six years ago. That ship sailed a long while back.

"If you need a wingman, just let me know."

Seth raised an eyebrow. "Dude, as you noticed, I'm gay. No offense, but you probably don't hang out at my kind of bar." Seth had been young enough when he enlisted that his experience with gay bars of any kind was limited.

Jesse shrugged. "My buddy Brent from school is gay. When we go out, I keep the girls away from him, and he distracts the guys from me. Works great."

"That's pretty cool," Seth admitted. "Good on you."

By the time the movie ended, Jesse was sleeping, leaning back into his corner of the couch with his eyes shut and his mouth open.

Seth smiled, overcome with affection as he thought about how much Jesse still looked like his much-younger self. He picked up their dishes and empty bottles and carried them out to the kitchen.

Jesse snored mightily, and Seth snickered. Rather than try to manhandle his brother to bed, Seth just tossed the crocheted throw over him. He figured Jesse would drag himself to his room when he woke up.

"'Night, Jesse," Seth said quietly, still needing to pinch himself to believe he was finally home.

He settled into bed and winced as his back spasmed. He'd already made an appointment with a chiropractor and booked a massage for his tight shoulders at a local chain—with a gift card from an overdue birthday present. *Just another souvenir that makes the war harder to forget.*

Sleep, when it came, did not come gently. Seth found himself back in Afghanistan, pinned down with his men and badly outnumbered. He smelled sulfur in the air from burning mines and felt the grit of sand everywhere.

He heard the whistle-whine of an air strike, felt the ground shake beneath his feet, and pulled a scarf over his mouth and nose to keep from choking on dust. The harsh staccato of gunfire and the screams of dying men made Seth's stomach knot as his heart thudded, wondering if each breath would be his last.

More explosions rocked the night, but everything around Seth had changed. Fire and smoke filled the end of a dark tunnel. He saw the form of a man limned in an unearthly green glow. Strange energy made his skin prickle and raised the hair on the back of his neck. Seth ran for his life, pushing someone ahead of him. The smell of dank stone and fresh blood raised bile in his throat.

Slick mud made running difficult. He shoved his companion toward the mouth of the tunnel, and they slip-slid toward safety. A blast behind them sent flames rushing through the darkness, and a rain of dirt and stone pelted them from overhead. Seth knew they had to reach the opening before the whole structure came down on top of them.

They got to the end, and Seth dragged his companion away from the entrance as the tunnel collapsed behind them with a rumble. He still couldn't see the face of the man who accompanied him, but the relief he felt that they were both safe and alive filled him so fully that he knew the stranger was important.

The scene changed to a hospital room. Seth lay in a bed, with IVs lacing his arms. A tall, thin man looked down at him. His long face, sharp features, and wire-rimmed glasses made him look like a humorless accountant. The man's arms were crossed over his chest, and on his right hand was a large ring with a blood-red stone.

Seth startled awake. His heart pounded, and his T-shirt clung to his back, wet with sweat. Disoriented, he looked wildly around him, and it took a while for him to believe that he was safe in his old room at home.

Where did the tunnel come from? Who was the man I saw inside it? What happened—and what was that glow?

The first answer his mind supplied was "magic," but Seth's rational side shot that down right away.

There's no such thing as magic. I must have seen something in a movie, and my brain glommed it onto stuff that happened over there.

Who was the "accountant," and why was I in the hospital? Do I know him?

He shook his head to clear it, confused and upset and repeated calming phrases to bring down his racing heartbeat. *I'm home. I'm safe. No one's trying to kill me.*

But even as Seth tried to reassure himself, a quiet voice in the back of his mind spoke up.

Are you sure?

4

EVAN

Evan's phone vibrated, a reminder to check in with Seth. He glanced at the time and frowned. Seth should have called or texted to touch base half an hour ago—he had definitely missed his check-in.

He probably hit pay dirt with the research and didn't hear his alarm or didn't set one, Evan thought. But just in case, he texted Seth.

Evan: *Find something interesting?*

When no snarky reply came within minutes, Evan hit speed dial. The phone rang until voice mail picked up.

Shit.

He didn't dare leave his research notes where someone could pry, so he jammed everything into his backpack and left the books on the table, hoping he'd be back soon.

Seth's phone might have died—but that doesn't seem likely. He could have moved somewhere that didn't have a good signal—but he made his previous check-in.

Every reason Evan could find for why he might be overreacting didn't hold up when he thought about it. *I knew we should have stayed together.*

The bad feeling in his belly grew to full-out foreboding when he saw an ambulance parked outside the library and followed the EMTs

49

to the same section where Seth had been researching. Neither the reference librarian nor Seth was anywhere to be seen.

He spotted Seth's messenger bag and notes in a glass-walled room. The door was locked when Evan tried to open it. The EMTs had ventured into the stacks, giving Evan the chance to retrieve Seth's belongings without having to explain anything. He held his hand over the lock, murmuring an *unlock* rote spell. The tumblers clicked, and Evan pulled the door open easily.

He shoved the papers and notebook into Seth's messenger bag and shouldered into his jacket, hoping no one wondered about him having both a backpack and another satchel.

Seth left his jacket in the room. The hex bags are gone, and so is his phone. He must have thought there was a threat.

Evan slipped back into the larger room and edged closer to the ambulance crew. An older woman sat on the floor, surrounded by medics and a worried library staffer.

"I must have fainted," she told them. "One minute I was looking for a book, and then I woke up on the floor, and Kevin called for help." The staffer, who was presumably Kevin, nodded in agreement.

Evan drew back before anyone saw him and made a quick check of the rest of the special reference room. Seth was nowhere to be found.

If he were here, he'd be the one who called in the librarian's situation, and he'd stay nearby.

Foreboding hardened into dread. He hadn't seen signs of a struggle in the glass-walled room, and nothing in the larger outer room looked amiss. Then he spotted something on the floor and his breath caught in fear: Seth's phone. He picked it up; the screen cracked but still working. *Seth wouldn't have left this behind willingly. He didn't make his check-in call, so he could have been taken any time in the last hour. Fuck.*

Evan hurried up the steps to the main level. Two uniformed police officers were coming his direction—and one of them was Derek Nelson.

He forced himself not to look at the cops and plastered a bland expression on his face, hoping Nelson would be so busy talking to his partner that he didn't recognize Evan. It almost worked. Nelson passed him, then stopped and backed up.

"You were one of the guys out by the observatory," Nelson said, giving Evan the once-over.

Evan managed a wan smile. "And now I'm at the library."

Nelson opened his mouth to say something, but his partner showed up beside him. "We need to go," he prompted and jerked his head in the direction of the stairs to the reference room.

Nelson turned his attention back to Evan. "Stay out of trouble," he warned, in a tone that made it clear he'd be expecting problems.

"I always try to," Evan replied, keeping his voice neutral and lengthening his stride. He resisted the urge to look over his shoulder and barely kept himself from running.

Fuck. He's got it in for us. So there's no way I can go to the cops if Seth really is missing.

He found their truck exactly where Seth parked it. The wardings would have prevented magical vandalism, and Evan couldn't see any physical damage. *But where's Seth?*

Evan dug his partner's phone out and looked through the call history. He saw the first check-in, and several texts Seth had sent to him with tidbits and photos he had found. Seth had uploaded his findings to the cloud, so Evan could check them when he got back to the RV.

One unsent text caught his eye, and he noted the time as well as the content—a picture of a building owned by Osborn that sat adjacent to an abandoned subway station.

Interesting...

He gave Seth's bag a quick check, something he hadn't taken time for back in the library. Evan had feared not being able to come back for Seth's things if the reference section got closed due to the librarian's accident. Now that he knew Officer Nelson responded to the call, he was doubly glad no one else had a chance to rifle through Seth's bag.

The knife is gone.

Evan knew that Seth wouldn't have removed the knife in a public place unless he believed he or someone else was in danger.

Did someone harm the librarian to get her out of the way? Or was she the bait to draw him out?

She wasn't bleeding.

A sudden fall should have left marks, a broken nose perhaps, or some other injury. The librarian looked flustered but unhurt.

Magic could make a person lose time and forget. He shivered, wondering if whoever had tracked them to the library had been looking specifically for Seth or if they had considered grabbing Evan first.

There were more people around where I was. Someone couldn't have taken me away without being noticed.

Evan circled the building, hoping to find anything that might explain Seth's sudden absence. Although he wished for evidence that Seth had followed someone suspicious, Evan felt increasingly sure that his partner had been kidnapped.

He found a rear door left ajar. When he followed the service corridor, it led to the back of the special reference section.

It wouldn't be easy to drag Seth out if he was unconscious, but if someone could handle him, they could take him out through here, and no one would be the wiser.

Evan hadn't seen blood near Seth's chair or anywhere along the back hallway. That just made him all the more certain magic was to blame.

He had both sets of keys to the truck—his own and Seth's from the messenger bag. At least he didn't have to hot-wire their vehicle. Evan chose to leave before Officer Nelson decided to blame him somehow for the librarian's fall.

Fear spiked through him for Seth's safety. *I don't have time to be afraid. I need to find Seth and bring him home.*

Evan drove to the campground by a roundabout route in case anyone tried to follow him. He parked the truck and checked the wardings on the RV, but nothing had been disturbed.

Once he got inside, Evan called Milo and Toby. "Seth's gone—and I think Osborn had something to do with it."

"Slow down," Milo said. Evan could hear Toby in the background urging him to put the call on speaker. "Start at the beginning."

Evan paced as he recounted everything that had happened. "We thought we were ahead of the game," Evan admitted. "And we thought we were being careful. We were just in the library. It's supposed to be safe. Kids go there, for fuck's sake."

"Everything you're saying sounds like someone whammied Seth," Toby replied. "And since you're on the witch disciple's home turf, it doesn't take much to figure out who."

"It doesn't help to have Nelson out to get us," Evan said. "Usually, we have some time before the cops notice us."

"Nelson's the next victim? Maybe Osborn or one of his minions passed along a 'helpful' tip—like a warning about troublemakers who were new in town. It takes a twisted sense of humor to pit him against the guys who are trying to save his life, but I wouldn't put it past Osborn," Milo added.

"I was nearly done with my research before everything fell apart—good thing, because I don't think I can go back there," Evan told them. "And I've got everything Seth found. We think we know where the anchor is—just not how to open the hiding place."

"I'm assuming you sent that photo of the seal to Teag and Travis? We couldn't come up with anything, but they've got connections. If anyone can figure it out, they will," Toby said.

"None of that matters if we can't find Seth." Evan knew the men could hear the worry in his voice.

"You will," Milo assured him. "This could be a good time to call in reinforcements."

"Can you—"

"Milo is in the hospital. I'm sitting with him right now," Toby said, and it sounded as if he'd taken the phone. Milo protested loudly, and Toby shushed his husband. "It's his heart again. They're running tests. It could be serious."

Milo bellowed his displeasure, and Toby must have covered the microphone with his hand, although Evan could still make out his words. "We can't leave," Toby said. "You know we would if we could. And no, I'm not going anywhere without you, you old coot."

"Milo's right. You belong there with him. Who do I need to call?" Evan's heart sank.

"We've got a connection for you. Name is Joe Mack. I told Seth about him. I'll text you his number. Mark Wojcik vouches for him, and that's good enough for me," Toby said. "Couple things you need to know. First—He's pretty much immortal."

"He's what? How did no one think to mention that before now?"

"Mack made a deal with some ancient Slavic god who saved his life and gives him magic. He's super strong, his skin can be metal for short periods, and he's almost impossible to kill," Toby continued.

"Okay," Evan replied, drawing out the syllables. "That could be handy."

"Mark says Joe is a stand-up kind of guy," Toby went on. "But he's also got friends in the Laveccia crime family. Old ties there, especially with their *strega*."

"What's that?"

"It's an Italian witch—someone with very strong magic," Milo chimed in, as if he needed Evan to know he wasn't out of the game.

"Maybe it wouldn't be such a bad idea to have a witch and a magical metal man in our corner if Osborn is this big of a threat," Evan conceded.

"You can't take the witch disciple on alone, and you're going to need help to get Seth if Osborn's the one who took him." Toby sounded worried.

"If Mack is an okay guy, why's he in bed with the Mob?"

"It's a long story," Toby replied. That Milo wasn't hijacking more of the conversation told Evan volumes about how the other man must be feeling.

"Mack is around a hundred and fifty years old—doesn't look it, so I hear. He's worked with the Laveccia *stregas* since the 1800s. The witches tend to be lone wolves—connected to the Family, but separate in their own way. Hold off on judging until you get a sense for him," Toby advised.

"If he can help me get Seth back, he could have horns and a tail for all I'd care."

"Don't joke about such things. You never know who's listening," Milo spoke up, utterly serious.

"It's still early. Let me call Mack and see what he has to say. If Osborn took Seth, we don't know how much time we've got."

"Evan—you can do this," Toby said. "You've got good instincts, and you're a fine hunter. Seth trained you well—and he's right to believe in you. I know you'll bring him back."

"I intend to," Evan replied, resolute. *No matter how many witchy sons of bitches I need to take down to do it.*

The call ended with admonitions from both sides to take care. Evan shoved the phone in his pocket and dropped onto the leather couch, then leaned forward with his head in his hands. The RV felt empty without Seth. Evan remembered the last time one of the witch disciples tried to snatch Seth and how he and some friends saved the day.

Osborn's holding all the cards. Does he know that Seth and I are both descendants of the deputies who killed Gremory? Did he grab Seth for a sacrifice instead of Nelson? Could I trade myself for Seth?

Evan knew Seth would never forgive him if he tried the last option, but Evan intended to consider every possibility.

We thought that knowing so much about Osborn before we came to Cleveland would make this a slam dunk. We got cocky, and now Seth's in danger.

Witches generally preferred a full moon for their rituals, a natural time of power. That was the only thing keeping Evan's panic in check. A quick look at his phone verified that they had several days left before then. If Osborn intended to sacrifice Seth instead of Nelson—which would decrease the power boost from the ritual—then he was unlikely to reduce the advantage even more by working the magic at the wrong time.

Think. Don't feel. There'll be time enough to feel when it's over.

"I'm coming for you, Seth. Hang on," he whispered. His thumb hovered over the phone number Teag sent him. Then he pressed and heard the call ring through to voice mail.

"My name is Evan Malone. I'm a hunter. Mark Wojcik says you can be trusted. I need your help. We should talk. Willis Osborn kidnapped my partner, and I intend to get him back. Call me."

Evan ended the call and hoped his voice didn't shake as much as his hand.

Seconds later, the phone rang. "We should meet," a gravelly voice said. "Come to the diner at Fifth and Main in an hour. Last booth on the right. Tell me your story, and I'll see if I can help."

"Thank you," Evan replied, assuming it to be Joe Mack.

"Don't thank me yet—I haven't done anything," the person replied and ended the call.

Evan stared at the phone, trying to collect his thoughts and quiet his emotions. Meeting with Joe would have terrified Evan a few months ago before he and Seth fought the Charleston witch disciple. They'd been supported in that fight by supernatural allies that included witches, psychics, a medium, root workers, and a vampire. After that, an immortal champion of a forgotten god didn't seem all that strange.

Man up, Malone. Gotta save my guy.

He forced himself to eat a bologna sandwich for a belated lunch, even though he hardly tasted it. Evan spent the time before his meeting with Joe sorting through what he and Seth had discovered at the library. Old photographs made a persuasive case for Osborn existing under many aliases for more than a century. The public records search provided clues to what Evan suspected were dummy corporations Osborn had used to buy and sell real estate through the decades without linking the properties directly to himself. Seth's map research raised some interesting possibilities of locations to check out.

They'd made progress, but at what cost?

Does Joe Mack know about Osborn? If Toby's right, Joe is even older. Do immortals who live in the same area keep track of each other? I'd think that they'd figure out who was suspiciously long-lived. Unless Joe's magic and Osborn's witchiness can hide them.

Evan knew that the only way to find out was to meet Joe at the diner. He grabbed his coat and headed for the door, pausing next to a photo fastened to the wall. In it, he and Seth stood with their arms around one another, laughing. The Blue Ridge Mountains stretched behind them, and the late afternoon sun gave the photograph a special glow.

"I'll find you," Evan promised Seth, staring at the photo. "I swear to God I will. Hang on. I'm coming."

Gus's Diner looked like it had been around forever. The 1940s vibe was original, not hipster retro. Evan wondered if that made it more comfortable for a man who still remembered that era.

He looked toward the rear booth and took a moment to size up his potential ally, who sat with his back to the wall as if expecting trouble.

For a man who was more than a century old, Joe Mack looked to be in his mid-thirties. He had a workingman's build, with broad shoulders and strong arms. Joe had blond hair, a wide face, and light blue eyes. He might not be handsome, but he looked dependable, maybe even trustworthy.

For Seth's sake, Evan hoped his first impression held true.

Evan strode to the rear booth and stopped beside the table. He figured that Joe had been sizing him up while he'd been taking Joe's measure.

"Joe Mack?" he asked.

"Guess you must be Evan. Have a seat." He gestured toward his half-empty coffee cup. "You want to order something?"

"Just coffee," Evan said as Joe signaled a server.

Once Evan had a steaming cup in front of him, Joe gave him another appraising look.

"You're younger than I expected."

"I hear you're older than you look."

Joe chuckled. "Wojcik tell you that?"

Evan shook his head. "Toby Cornell, and Milo."

"They're good people." Joe took a sip of coffee. "So, what's your problem?"

Evan glanced around, but no one was seated close enough to overhear. He decided to take a flying leap of faith for Seth's sake and be completely honest. Joe listened without interrupting and didn't act as if any part was too fantastic to be believed.

"The two of you have stopped four of these bastards?" Joe asked when Evan finished.

"Seth trained before he set out on his...quest," Evan replied. "And after the first witch disciple, allies helped us with the other cases."

"But you came to Cleveland without backup?"

Evan shook his head. "We expected to connect with Mark Wojcik or

Travis Dominick since they're not far from here. But everything moved faster than we thought it would. I guess Osborn was as ready for us as we thought we were ready for him."

"Willis Osborn is a snake," Joe said. "I knew he was a witch. Cleveland has plenty of those. I don't know what you've heard, but I don't have a beef with everyone with supernatural abilities. I'm not the police. I'm not even the Supernatural Secret Service."

"I didn't think you were. But I could use an ally. Especially one who knows the territory." Evan felt his gut tighten. If Joe wouldn't help, he could still turn to Mark and Travis.

"What's your plan?"

"Find Seth, steal the anchor, stop Osborn from killing his next victim, and cause his ritual to fail," Evan replied, thinking how deceptively simple it sounded, and how dangerous and complicated—and insane—it was.

"What happens when the ritual fails?"

"Each of the witch disciples chose one of the deputies' families to be his victims. When he works the ritual with his true sacrifice, it opens up some kind of rift where Gremory's spirit is trapped. Then the disciple can steal power from Gremory, and the energy from the blood sacrifice keeps Gremory trapped. If the witch disciple uses a different victim, the spell isn't as effective."

"You and Seth are both victims that got away," Joe said.

Evan nodded. "Seth saved my life. But one of the witch disciples killed Seth's brother by mistake. Seth didn't know how to find the warlock at the time, but we intend to go back for him. He won't get away with murder."

The edge in Evan's voice must have registered with Joe, because he seemed to regard Evan a little differently.

"How is it that the murders have gone on for a century and no one noticed?"

Evan shrugged. "No one bothered to look too closely. The warlocks usually hide their kills. The families know there are 'accidental' deaths, but no one looks for a pattern, so they don't see it. The cops don't believe in magic. So, it went on."

"I've had my eye on Osborn—but not for killing those relatives.

Didn't know about that part. He's involved in other things that are just as bad," Joe replied.

"The witch in Charleston was trafficking shifters and psychics. Apparently that's been going on for a while, under the radar. Some of our allies are working to stop that, but it's slow going," Evan said.

Joe nodded. "Good to know. I'll keep an eye out now that you've told me. But Osborn's a little different. He was an apothecary, and he was badly hurt when he was thrown from a horse—long before he became a powerful witch. He depended on the drugs he compounded, and I suspect he turned to magic when the medicine wasn't enough. He may also need to draw energy from his sacrifices to deal with his injury."

"That's a good theory. But it doesn't seem to have made him more vulnerable."

"Just because you can't see the weakness doesn't mean it isn't there," Joe replied.

Evan knew he wasn't hiding his restlessness well, feeling jittery without Seth. "The ritual would be strongest at the full moon. We've got to find Seth before then. I'd like your help—but I'm going after him one way or another."

Joe gave him a look that Evan wasn't sure how to decipher. "You intend to go, with or without help?"

Evan met his gaze without flinching. "I know you come from a different time. Maybe this is hard to hear. But I love Seth. I'll do whatever it takes to save him."

Joe chuckled. "Some things weren't spoken of openly, but they existed. I'm much harder to shock than you think. You should have seen the Roaring Twenties."

"If it was like *The Great Gatsby*, I'll pass."

Joe's laugh rumbled like thunder. "Good point." He sobered. "I'll help. But we need to do this smart. Are you staying somewhere safe?"

Evan nodded. "The truck and RV are warded. I'm as safe there as I could be anywhere."

"Then go home and stay there. I need to talk to a witchy friend of mine. He'll know how to take on an enemy like Osborn."

"I'll give you one day," Evan countered. "I won't risk Seth's life by delaying."

"And he wouldn't want you to throw your life away by running into a fight half-assed."

Evan thought he was holding his own pretty well in a stare-down with an immortal servant of a god. "You have my phone number."

"I'll call you. We'll find a way to get Seth back."

EVAN NEEDED TO CLEAR HIS HEAD AFTER MEETING WITH JOE, AND HE WAS hungry. He spotted a fast-food drive-through and figured that he was probably safe for the time it took to eat a burger.

His mind spun with his conversation with Joe, and his worry for Seth, drumming his fingers on the steering wheel as he waited for his burger, fries, and Coke.

Evan's phone rang, and he didn't check the number, hoping Joe was ready to get started right away.

"Evan?" the caller asked hesitantly.

"Parker, is that you?"

My brother.

5

SETH

"Vacation?" Seth echoed. He hadn't finished his first cup of morning coffee yet, and although he didn't have any firm plans, going on a spur-of-the-moment trip felt oddly wrong.

His mom nodded. "Before you get tied down with a job, we thought it would be a great idea if the whole family took the first trip in the RV to break it in. Jesse's already earned some time off."

Jesse came into the kitchen and flopped down in a chair beside Seth, intentionally jostling his arm to make the coffee slosh.

"Asshole," Seth muttered, rolling his eyes. He knew Jesse heard the affection in his tone.

"Takes one to know one," Jesse replied blithely.

Linda looked at Seth archly. "What did you call your brother?"

"Casserole," Seth replied, with a wide-eyed expression of innocence that had never worked on his skeptical mother.

"Uh-huh," Linda replied, obviously not believing a word of it.

"Where do you want to go?" Jesse asked. "Canada? Key West? Colorado?"

Linda laughed. "We weren't thinking anything quite that ambitious until your father gets the hang of driving the new truck and the fifth-wheeler. Together they're the length of a bus. We thought we might go to Richmond. There's a lot to see, we've never been there, I've always wanted to go, and it's far enough away to feel like a vacation."

Jesse shrugged. "Sounds good to me. Last trip before I have to pay my own way!"

"Moocher," Seth teased.

"Suck-up," Jesse returned.

Linda laughed and shook her head. "Seriously? You boys will be the death of me."

"When did you want to leave?" Seth asked. Something tugged at him to stay in Brazil. The dark-haired man he had glimpsed came to mind, and he figured it had been too long since he'd gotten laid if he was fixating on a stranger whose face he hadn't even seen.

"Saturday," she said. "Your dad wants to take the rig out on some short drives to get a feel for how it handles and how fast it goes through gas. I need to outfit it, so we have sheets and towels and kitchen stuff. Plus groceries. Think about what you want to bring—your gaming stuff should work, and it's got Wi-Fi."

"Sweet," Jesse said. "That means I can beat your ass on video games from here to the coast!"

Linda sighed and shook her head. "Language!" she chided, mostly teasing.

Seth gave her a playful side-eye. "You do know I spent six years learning to swear like a soldier, right?"

"I try not to think about any of that." She looked wistful. "You're home now and safe. That's all that matters."

Seth didn't fight the overwhelming urge he had to lean close and give his mother a kiss on the cheek. "That's for all the times I wanted to and couldn't," he said, surprised that the thought made tears spring to his eyes.

She turned and pressed a kiss to the top of his head. "I missed you too."

Jesse cleared his throat and flung his arms wide. "Hey, what about me? I'm right here!"

Linda gave Jesse a fond look of exasperation. "I know that. It's why the groceries disappear into thin air."

Seth guffawed and gave Jesse a backhanded slap to the chest. "She's got you on that!"

"Boys," she said, shaking her head.

"Sounds like a plan," Seth replied. He wasn't enthusiastic for the trip itself, but after six years overseas, he craved time with his family.

Jesse clapped him on the shoulder. "I've got plans for you, bro. A lot can happen in two days!"

After breakfast, Jesse and Seth went out to Jesse's Mustang. "I've been thinking of the things I wanted to show you."

"Like what?" Seth couldn't help being pleased that Jesse had planned time for them to spend together and was surprised that he'd managed to get the time off from his job.

Jesse grinned, a broad smile Seth remembered from their childhood when Jesse found something that lit a fire inside him.

"Well, there's a mega-arcade with retro games over at the new entertainment complex in Terre Haute," Jesse said. "It's also got mini-golf. I've found some really good places to eat. And if you're interested, I'd like to show you the campus."

Seth smiled. "I'd love all of that." He had told Jesse many times how proud he was of him for going after his degree. Seth was only now putting together his plan for what he wanted to do. Just getting home alive had been a big enough challenge.

"And we'll end the day at the best steakhouse in Terre Haute," Jesse promised. "My treat."

Seth raised an eyebrow. "Oh yeah? They pay you that much? How are you suddenly made of money?"

"I'm an international man of mystery," Jesse whispered. "If I told you where I got the money, I'd have to kill you."

"All right, James Bond. Show me what you've got in mind," Seth joked.

They spent the morning at the sports complex, going from the retro video arcade to the batting cages to mini-golf. For lunch, Jesse took him to his favorite ramen shop.

"My friends and I loved this place," he said as they slurped fresh noodles from a spicy broth. "It's cheap and filling. That's big with the college crowd."

"This is...amazing," Seth said with food in his mouth. "So good."

Jesse laughed. "Didn't they feed you in the Army?"

"Not like this."

Seth had missed the easy camaraderie between the two of them; falling back into the give and take like no time had passed was a balm to his soul.

"Just wait until we go to the steakhouse," Jesse replied.

"You've been there?"

"On a date. It lives up to its reputation," Jesse assured him.

"You said you didn't have time to date. Let's hear details. You've been holding out on me."

Jesse blushed. "School took most of my time. But...I went out now and again. Still do."

Seth grinned. "Tell me more."

Jesse sighed. "Not much to tell. I've gone out with a few girls since I graduated, no one special. Maybe this is the year I get lucky. How about you?" He nudged Seth with his elbow. "Come on, tell me everything."

"The Army hasn't really caught up with the times," Seth said. "I didn't have much opportunity to date."

"Then now's a great time to make up for it," Jesse replied. "Brazil might not be very progressive, but Terre Haute's better. I bet you could find a date if you tried hard," he teased. "You're not hopeless."

"Gee, thanks."

Seth wasn't going to admit that for three nights straight, he'd dreamed of the dark-haired stranger. Each time, he'd woken hard and desperate, and while he'd remembered the erotic parts of his dreams, Seth always felt like the most important elements slipped out of reach.

After lunch they went to the local brewery and then took in a matinee at the 1920's era theater. Jesse drove them around campus, pointing out the highlights. Seth thought he glimpsed the dark-haired man from his dream. But once again, the stranger disappeared into the crowd before Seth could find him. He tried to shake off the mood that caused a weird combination of disappointment and foreboding.

Maybe I'm losing my mind.

Seth forced the thoughts away and threw himself into enjoying the plans Jesse made for them, which included wandering through the art museum and taking in a sprint car qualifier at the track.

"You should be an event planner," Seth said, in awe of Jesse's itinerary. "You've packed a month into several hours."

"I've had a lot of time to plan."

Seth had thought about coming home so many times and how he wanted to celebrate. He'd also come up with plenty of things for the two of them to do, craving a chance to get to know his brother again after his time away.

"Did you have other ideas?" Seth asked.

"Plenty. I want to go on ghost hunts. There's supposed to be a hell gate bridge. I want to go do a video there."

Something twisted hard and cold inside Seth. "Um, maybe not," he said, unable to shake the dread that chilled his marrow. Everything told him not to go to that bridge, and he had no idea why.

Jesse looked a little spooked. "Sure. There's plenty of other stuff to do. Indianapolis isn't that far away. Or Chicago."

Seth nodded. "Good. That's all...good."

"You okay?" Jesse gave him a quizzical look.

"Yeah. Just...you know that phrase about feeling like someone walked over your grave?" Seth shivered. "Kinda had that a moment ago."

Jesse clapped him on the shoulder. "Let's fix that right now." He took Seth on an off-the-cuff walking tour, pointing out local landmarks, meandered through a local park, and stopped at a place Jesse assured him served the best ice cream in Indiana.

Going places and doing things was fun, but what Seth liked the most was spending time with his brother and having Jesse's full attention.

Despite the ice cream, Seth's stomach rumbled.

"Hungry?" Jesse asked and checked the time on his phone. "By the time we get to the steakhouse, our reservation should be ready. We've got a bit of a walk to the car. Let's go."

Seth enjoyed seeing Jesse's idea of a perfect day and gave his brother credit for the playful sense of adventure he brought to the itinerary.

The smell of grilled meat and wood smoke filled the air when they parked beside a stacked stone building that had clearly been a landmark for quite some time.

"This place is famous locally for its prime rib, but all its steaks are good," Jesse assured him. They walked inside, and Seth saw a large stone fireplace with a roaring fire. The decor looked comfortable and homey, without all the brass and steel common in upscale chain restaurants. Jesse checked in at the host station, and Seth couldn't help noticing how much Jesse had grown up.

The server led them to a table for four in a quiet corner. "Wait until you see the menu," Jesse told him. "Great stuff."

To Seth's surprise, the menu was both extensive and reasonably priced. He and Jesse ordered prime rib, which came with huge baked potatoes and a shared side of grilled asparagus. Over dinner, Jesse told him more about his time at college and then his job, and Seth enjoyed hearing about the drama of campus life and his brother's accomplishments.

Jesse asked about what it had been like on deployment. Seth answered truthfully, but glossed over the worst experiences, the things that were difficult to explain to civilians, and the memories that fueled his nightmares.

"I learned combat skills from the soldiers I served with," Seth told him. "And the computer stuff they taught me will pay off with the security company I want to start. But if I had it to do over again, I wouldn't have gone. It changed me, and I'll never be able to change back."

The sympathy in Jesse's eyes told Seth he was forgiven for his impulsive enlistment. "No matter what you did, you wouldn't be the same person you were six years ago. Everyone changes. But you're still my brother. And I'm very glad to have you home."

Seth didn't think he could possibly have room for dessert, but the tray of homemade cheesecake slices looked too good to pass up. They placed their orders and asked for coffee to go with it.

"You won't regret having dessert," Jesse told him as they waited. "If you feel guilty about eating it, we can go on a hike tomorrow."

"Jesse?" A voice sounded behind Seth, and he turned to see a good-looking black-haired man approaching with a grin.

"Taylor! Come meet my brother," Jesse said, waiving the newcomer over. "Have dessert with us."

Taylor held out his hand to Seth. "I'm Taylor Greer. You must be Seth. I've heard a lot about you."

Seth didn't miss the way the man checked him out. He shifted in his chair, flattered but uncomfortable at having someone cruise him in front of his brother.

"Nice to meet you," Seth replied. "How do you know Jesse?"

"We work together; started at the same time. And we both were part of the RPG club back in college," Taylor answered. "I'm a bit older than the other guys in our class because I took a couple of years off to work. Jesse always talked about his big brother. I'm happy to meet you."

Taylor slid into the empty seat beside Seth and turned inward to face both brothers. "So, how long are you in town for?" he asked Seth.

"Don't know for sure yet," Seth replied. "A while, if I'm lucky."

"Seth wants to start his own computer security business," Jesse volunteered, sounding like a proud mom.

"Interesting choice." Taylor looked at Seth. "How did you come up with that?"

Seth shrugged. "I did a lot of that sort of thing in the military. Figured I'd put my experience to good use."

"Taylor's a systems engineer," Jesse said, nudging their conversation along. "Figured you two might have a lot to talk about."

The server brought their desserts, and Taylor asked for a cup of coffee. As they ate, Jesse and Taylor told funny stories about campus life. Taylor also had plenty of amusing tales from the summers he had been a camp counselor at a wilderness retreat for LGBTQ youth. That confirmed Seth's suspicion that Taylor had given him the once-over.

Admittedly, my gaydar is a little rusty.

"Since this is my treat, I'm going to go settle the bill," Jesse announced, standing up. "Take your time. I want to order some cheesecake to take home for Mom and Dad."

Jesse's tone was nonchalant, but Seth had been reading his brother's tells since they were kids and knew when he wasn't telling the whole truth. Something clicked in Seth's mind, and he realized that Taylor's appearance was not as spontaneous as it seemed.

That little fart set me up on a blind date.

"It's great to finally meet you. I'm happy to show you around if you'd like," Taylor said with a welcoming smile.

"Sure," Seth replied. "Although Jesse's done a fine job."

"I'm sure he has, but I might bring a different perspective." Taylor's knee bumped Seth's under the table, a light touch there and gone, but a signal sent, nonetheless.

"We're taking a trip with our folks, but maybe we can meet up afterward," Seth answered. Taylor was cute and funny and seemed like a nice guy. Despite his initial annoyance at being maneuvered into the situation, Seth realized Jesse was trying to do a good thing.

Then why do I feel like I'm being unfaithful to consider going out with Taylor?

Taylor handed Seth his phone. "Text yourself, and then I'll have your number, and you'll have mine. I'll want to hear all about that trip —and how the two of you survive going on the great American vacation with your parents!"

When they said goodbye, Taylor held on to Seth's hand a few seconds longer than necessary and let go with a slide of fingers across his palm.

"Remember what I said about the road trip," Taylor told them. "Pictures or it didn't happen!" He waved and then sauntered off in the opposite direction from where they'd parked.

Seth gave Jesse a playful punch on the shoulder.

"Hey! What's that for? I just bought you steak and cheesecake!"

"And set me up on a blind date."

Jesse grinned. "Figured that out, did you? I always said you were smarter than you look," he teased with a fond tone.

Seth lightly smacked the back of Jesse's head. "Shut up."

"Make me."

"What are you, twelve?"

They laughed all the way back to Jesse's car. Seth couldn't have imagined a better homecoming.

〜

"Everyone's got their phones, wallets, and chargers?" Linda asked two days later when they were all in the truck.

"Did you remember to pee? I'm not pulling over five minutes onto the road. This rig isn't fun to park," Brian grumbled.

"You do know we're not ten, right, Dad?" Jesse said from the back seat where he and Seth were packed in with a drink cooler, two grocery bags of snacks, and enough handheld electronics to get them to Richmond.

"Everyone pees," Brian replied. "Just do it now before we leave so we don't have to stop right away. Do you remember that time—"

"Yes!" Seth and Jesse said in unison to forestall one of their dad's embarrassing vacation stories.

"We're good," Seth assured him. "Convoys didn't stop, either."

"That's why God planted bushes beside highways," Jesse said.

"Just drive, Brian." Linda shook her head. "The more things change, the more they stay the same."

Seth and Jesse exchanged a triumphant grin at having annoyed their parents, and Seth felt the weight of the past decade slip from his shoulders.

They stopped at a campground somewhere in West Virginia, halfway to Richmond. Linda shooed them all out of the RV until she could arrange the kitchen to her liking. Brian connected the utilities and then went for a walk to stretch his legs.

Seth and Jesse headed to the arcade, part of the camp's community building, next to the snack bar and convenience store.

"Kinda fun to come back when we can play as long as we want, huh?" Seth asked.

"Less stressful now that we don't have to beg Mom for quarters," Jesse agreed. "Although she'll probably freak if she finds out we loaded up on candy."

Seth chuckled. "If she's making dinner, you can count on that."

Jesse bought their favorites and tucked the bags and bars into his coat pockets. "Then we'll sneak them in, just like I snuck in a couple of bottles of whiskey."

"You do realize how silly that is. We're both over twenty-one," Seth reminded him.

"Explain that to Mom. She still fusses. But there's not too much she can say—I saw Dad sneaking a few bottles in too," Jesse said.

"You really think she doesn't know? When did anything happen that she didn't know about? She's just humoring us. Mom knows it's more fun if she pretends we got one over on her."

Seth's phone buzzed with a text, and he glanced at it. "Dinner's ready. We'd better go."

"Race you!" Jesse took off as soon as they were out of the door. Seth jogged the distance instead of running. "I win!"

Seth shrugged. "Who's sweaty, and who isn't? I'd say that's a win for me," he replied with a cocky grin.

The smell of meatloaf filled the camper as Linda pulled the pan from the oven. "Wash up and sit down," she said without looking up as they entered.

Seth waited his turn for the small bathroom. He opened a drawer looking for hand cream and recoiled when he saw a handgun inside.

"What the fuck?" he muttered. "Mom! Why is there a gun in the bathroom?"

The others came running, crowding into the small space outside. "What are you talking about?" Linda demanded. "What gun? We don't own a gun."

Seth opened the drawer and pointed. "That gun."

Brian looked at him, worried. "Son, there's nothing in there."

Seth stared into the empty drawer. "There was a gun in that drawer a few seconds ago. And not my service piece."

Brian laid a hand on Seth's shoulder. "Let's go eat. Everything's better with a full belly."

Linda gave Seth a worried look and headed for the kitchen. Jesse hung back until they were gone. "What's going on?"

"Later," Seth replied, closing the drawer and opening it several times to assure himself that the gun wouldn't magically appear.

Seth couldn't shake the feeling that everything about the fifth-wheeler was slightly wrong. He'd been inside a few times out of curiosity before they left home, and each visit reinforced his conviction that the trailer *should* have been different.

There were photos set around that aren't here. The bedspread ought to be another color. Something isn't right.

"Seth?" Linda sounded worried.

"Coming!" He hurried back to the table where the others were waiting. Linda had made a plate for him, and he took a seat next to Jesse.

"I'm sorry. I don't want to worry you. It's hard, coming back," Seth said and looked down. Better to let them think he had a raging case of PTSD than that he might be going slowly mad, assaulted by false memories.

"No harm done." Brian sounded a bit too chipper. "We're here for you. Maybe after six years in a hot zone, your brain doesn't feel safe without a weapon, so it conjured one up for you. Our minds do strange things."

"Maybe so," he replied, although he didn't believe it.

Linda and Jesse steered the conversation back to the drive and the places they'd seen that day.

"I've got plans for what we can see in Richmond," Jesse told them.

"You and Seth can do your own thing once we arrive," Linda said. "That's why we've got your Hayabusa on the rear rack. We'll uncouple the truck. There's a botanical garden and a couple of old mansions I want to see, plus the art museum."

"And the NASCAR track," Brian prompted.

"Of course." Linda patted his arm.

After Seth and Evan cleared the dishes, they went outside. The night had grown cold enough to see their breath.

"Talk to me, bro. You're scaring me a little. Not scared *of* you. Scared *for* you," Jesse said.

"I'm scaring me too, so you'll have to take a number."

They fell silent, and Jesse waited him out.

"I keep feeling like I came back *wrong*," Seth started, not sure how to put his feelings and premonitions into words. "Like the me who went overseas isn't the same me who's here now."

"None of us are the same people we were six years ago," Jesse replied. "We didn't change as much because we stayed here. Makes sense you'd feel more of a difference."

Seth shook his head. "That's not what I mean. I feel like maybe in a different time and place, *I* was different. But that's crazy talk."

Jesse seemed to take him seriously. "Maybe—maybe not. Lots of strange things turn out to be real. I'll help you figure this out."

Seth's surprise at the relief he felt overwhelmed him. "Thank you for believing in me."

"That's what brothers are for."

That night Seth dreamed about the strange hospital room. He'd been hurt a few times in the Army, but this didn't look like a military facility, and he didn't remember having been sent to a civilian hospital.

The same sharp-featured "accountant" stared down at him. Seth saw the man's mouth move, but heard nothing. The man regarded Seth in his hospital bed, but there was no compassion in his eyes. The red stone in his ring caught the light and glowed with an inner fire.

For a moment, Seth felt panic, and then lethargy swept over him, and he plunged back into sleep.

When he dreamed again, Seth was making love to the dark-haired stranger. He took his lover from behind, so he didn't see the man's face. Soft waves of chestnut brown hid his features, even when Seth tangled his fingers in his lover's hair as he thrust hard into his tight channel.

He swore the location was the master bedroom in the RV, but in the dream, it was their space and no one else's. Seth's body was clearly on board, and the fantasy left him hard and aching.

Since Seth and Jesse slept in the convertible beds that were part of the living room, the arrangement offered no privacy to jerk off and slake his desire. Seth watched Jesse for a moment to make sure his brother was still asleep, fearing he had made noise in his nightmare that woke the others. When Jesse continued to snore, Seth crept to the bathroom.

Mindful of the trailer's thin walls, he slicked up his hand with hand cream from the medicine cabinet where his brain swore Astroglide used to sit. Seth pushed his boxer-briefs down his thighs and cupped his balls with his left hand while he tugged on his stiff cock with his right.

Dark brown hair. Hazel eyes. Still can't make out the rest of his features. Should be able to pick my lover out of a lineup. That wasn't the first time we've made love. We knew too much about what makes the other person fall apart.

"*Evan,*" he whispered as he came.

JESSE AND SETH HEADED INTO DOWNTOWN RICHMOND EARLY THE NEXT morning. They drove down Monument Avenue, remarking on the statues that had recently been relocated and the empty spaces left behind. Jesse downloaded a walking tour to his phone, and they explored the area around the Capitol and then the trendy Fan District.

"This place ranked the best for lunch plus local atmosphere," Jesse told Seth as they stopped in front of a tall, old brick building that had been repurposed from some kind of warehouse. "It's supposed to be a pretty great place for cocktails and trivia nights too."

The sign read *Tredegar's*. Seth felt another stab of déjà vu. "Treddy's," he murmured, knowing that the place was important, but not why.

Jesse looked at him sideways. "Yeah, that's what the locals call it. How did you know?"

Seth shook his head. "I just did. Let's go in."

The interior was a mix of wrought iron railings, brass fixtures, white twinkle lights, and exposed brick with wooden ceiling beams, a trendy but welcoming environment that didn't take itself too seriously. Seth scanned the customers, on edge as if he expected trouble. Then he searched the faces of the servers at the bar, with a desperate longing that choked him with sadness.

"Seth?" Jesse put a hand on his shoulder. "We can go somewhere else if you'd like."

Seth shook his head. "No. I'm fine. It's a pretty place."

The food was as good as promised, and both of them made short work of barbecue sandwiches, sweet potato fries, fried pickles, and a side of Brunswick stew, washed down with locally-brewed beer. The silences had become as relaxed as the conversation between them, and Seth took comfort in being able to pretend for a few minutes that he had never left.

Seth picked up the tab this time, and Jesse promised to spring for ice cream. Full and relaxed, they waited for their bill.

He spotted a familiar figure near the bar. "I'll be back," Seth told Jesse, moving so quickly that he nearly knocked over a server. He kept the dark-haired man in view as he wove through the crowd and found him playing with his phone next to the bar.

Before Seth had a chance to figure out what to say, the man glanced up, giving Seth a good look at his face. Seth felt a shock of recognition, followed by a wave of bewilderment. The features were intimately familiar, but Seth had no idea who he was.

"You don't belong here; you need to run," the stranger said.

Someone in the crowd jostled Seth hard enough that he stumbled. When he looked up, the stranger was gone.

"Are you okay?" Jesse asked, coming up behind him.

"Yeah." Seth stared at the empty spot at the bar where the stranger had been just seconds ago. "I'm fine." *I'm losing my marbles.*

Jesse clapped him on the shoulder as they stepped back onto the sidewalk. "Come on—I've got something pretty interesting to show you." They walked for a while and turned onto Church Street. To Seth's surprise, Jesse led him through another restaurant and out back to their patio.

"You're hungry again?" Seth asked, unsure what they were doing there.

"Hungry for a scare, maybe." Jesse pointed to a huge wooden door that blocked off what looked to be an old passageway. "I told you I wanted to look up some spooky spots. That's one end of the Church Street Tunnel, built for a railroad a hundred years ago. There was a collapse, and a train never made it out. It's still buried in there—along with its crew. Locals say it's haunted."

"Doesn't seem to hurt the restaurant's business," Seth said, trying to hide how uncomfortable the tunnel made him.

"Maybe this isn't the haunted end. The other side isn't blocked off until a couple hundred feet into the tunnel. There's a rickety fence, but you can see inside quite a way. From the pictures I found, it looks like it's down a hill in a wooded area, but if you want to explore, we can come back with better shoes."

"No!" Seth spoke sharply enough that Jesse's eyebrows rose in surprise. He shook his head. "We shouldn't. It's dangerous." He could barely put the urgency he felt into words, the utter certainty that they should stay the hell away.

"Okay. We don't have to. We'd probably get all muddy anyhow," Jesse said in a tone like he was talking to a spooked horse. "Mom would kill us if we got the RV dirty."

"I'm sorry," Seth said, feeling his face color with embarrassment. "I must be cracking up."

Jesse bumped his shoulder. "It's okay. There's lots of other stuff to do. And we don't have that long before dinner. Tomorrow, we could drive down to Virginia Beach. It's not far, and I've always wanted to see the ocean."

Seth appreciated the peace offering, and he nodded enthusiastically. "I think that sounds fantastic. Come on—let's walk some more before we head back."

To Seth's relief, Jesse kept the conversation light. He knew they would have to talk more about his nightmares and his growing obsession with the stranger—*Evan*—he seemed to see everywhere.

Seth just hoped that by the time they had that conversation, he had a clue about what the fuck was going on.

6

EVAN

"PARKER?" EVAN'S EMOTIONS WHIPSAWED WITH JUST ONE WORD. LOVE, anger, grief, disappointment, and hope all washed over him like a tide that might pull him under.

"It's been a while," the voice replied.

"Couple of months, at least. A lot has happened." Evan listened closely to the caller, trying to match the voice of the man to the teen he had been so close to before he'd fled their home. Parker was four years younger, so he'd been thirteen the last time Evan had seen him in person. The deeper voice reminded Evan that Parker would be twenty now.

After Evan left home, Parker had to sneak sending emails, so their parents didn't find out. That meant their contact had been haphazard, but Evan treasured every word. They had managed to stay in touch every month or so, until this past year when Evan had gone on the road with Seth and everything changed.

Parker cleared his throat. "Yeah. Too long."

Anger threatened to bubble up, Evan's first line of defense in those first lonely years after he left home. So much had been left unsaid and unfinished. He reined in his temper, trying not to lash out.

MORGAN BRICE

"Why haven't you called?" Evan tried and failed to keep his voice neutral.

"You didn't call either."

Evan took a deep breath and let it out. "This last year...it's been unusual. There were some things that I didn't want to drag you into."

Parker paused. "Are you okay?"

Evan felt a stab of hurt thinking of how *not okay* he was with Seth's disappearance. "Yeah," he lied. "Things are going pretty well now." *That much was true until Seth vanished.* "How about you?"

"I left."

"What?"

Pride colored Parker's tone. "I finally grew a pair and left home. I couldn't stand being there anymore—the house, the state, the church. I'm out—for good."

"Congratulations." Evan felt proud and worried. "Do you need money? Are you staying somewhere safe? Do you have a job?"

"I'm sharing an apartment, which keeps the rent down. I'm working several jobs to save money to go to community college. Things are tight, but I'm getting by," Parker replied, sounding pleased with himself.

"That's great. It sounds like you're really making it happen," Evan praised, relieved that his brother had finally left the toxic environment they'd been raised in. Evan knew it stifled Parker, even if he wasn't gay.

Parker was quiet long enough that Evan checked to be sure the call hadn't ended. "Dad's sick. Cancer. I thought you'd want to know."

Evan wasn't prepared for the stab of old pain those words brought. "I don't know what to say," he admitted. "I know what I'm *supposed* to say—but it wouldn't be true. Dad was going to send me for conversion therapy or throw me out. Even Mom didn't try to defend me or stop him."

"They're leaning on me pretty hard to come home," Parker admitted. "And they wanted me to pressure you. I'm not. Just letting you know. What you do is up to you."

"Is he sorry?" Evan heard the brittle edge in his voice, the line between rage and heartbreak.

Seth's missing and in danger. Now this. I know where my priorities lie.

"Mom says you need to come home and make peace with him."

"Fuck that. I was seventeen when they rejected me, Parker. I barely had time to pack a bag. I was lucky—I didn't end up dead or trafficked, like a lot of kids who get thrown away. So, if he doesn't regret what he did, I've got nothing to say to him."

"Mom's taking this hard. She says she needs you."

"To clean up whatever mess Dad's going to leave behind? The answer is no. Let Jim help them." Evan pinched the bridge of his nose, feeling a headache coming on. "Hell, I'm probably already disinherited, for whatever that's worth."

"I never forgave them for making you leave," Parker said.

Once upon a time, Evan and Parker had been inseparable. The four years' difference between their ages never seemed to matter. There had only been one secret Evan kept from Parker, and that was when he'd figured out he was gay. Back then, Evan was struggling hard enough to accept himself without the shame and guilt his very conservative church claimed he deserved. He was afraid that if Parker knew, it would change everything.

"Look, this is a bad time. Maybe we can talk again later?" Evan couldn't focus, but he didn't want to push Parker away since he'd worked up the nerve to call.

"Okay," Parker said, sounding uncertain. "I'd like that."

Evan ended the call, overwhelmed by a tumult of emotions. Fear for Seth's safety was the strongest. Anger at his father came second. Despite everything, Evan regretted that he and Parker hadn't seen each other in person for so long and that their calls had grown more sporadic. Concern about his father's condition barely registered, which sparked guilt. Evan pushed those feelings down remorselessly. He also noted that Parker hadn't mentioned their brother Jim, most likely because he hadn't changed either, and Evan wasn't about to ask.

Dad has Mom, Jim, and the church he loved more than his oldest son. Let them care for him. He'd rather spit in my eye than have me come to say goodbye.

His phone rang again, and this time he recognized Joe Mack's number. "What did you find out?"

"Meet me at the speakeasy below the Hathaway Theater," Joe replied, not exactly answering his question.

"Why do we need to meet in a bar?"

"Not a bar—a speakeasy. In this case, an authentic one. I have new information, and we need to plan carefully to get Seth back alive."

"Alright. When?"

"Give me an hour to make some calls. I know you're edgy, and I realize that Seth's in danger. I think this will help. I'm asking you to trust me."

"See you then."

Evan swore under his breath as he pocketed the phone. *I can't go charging in after Seth by myself, even if I had a clue about where he is. I need Joe's help—and if he has friends, that's even better. We don't know how much time Seth has left. We've got to hurry.*

He drove to the address Joe Mack provided and found himself standing in front of a classic theater. It had been well-maintained despite its age, and Evan wondered how different it might have looked in its prime.

Evan read the marquee and recognized the movie currently playing was a gay romcom indie film. *Interesting place. I wonder how Joe is tied up with all this?*

He walked into the theater's foyer and found the corridor that led down the basement steps to a nondescript door. As Joe had instructed, he gave the coded knock.

It seemed like something out of a movie. A panel slid back, and he could see the doorman's eyes.

"Joe Mack sent me," Evan said, impatient with the procedures. *Seth's in trouble. We don't have time for this.*

The door opened. Evan felt like he had been transported back to the 1920s. The speakeasy's days of serving bootleg liquor were long past, but the hidden bar's vibe radiated the Roaring Twenties. An elaborate back bar with a huge mirror and ornately carved wood provided a focal point. The bar itself was just as massive and impressive.

Behind the bar, a good-looking man with black hair and gray eyes spared a glance for him as he entered. He cocked his head to the right. "Joe's that way."

"Thanks," Evan said, searching for his contact. The rest of the speakeasy was mostly empty, with just a few patrons at the bar. A grand piano dominated one side of the room, silently awaiting its pianist. It didn't take much imagination for Evan to picture the whole place filled with flappers and well-dressed gents, all fearful of a bust by the G-men.

Joe waved Evan over. His companions weren't what Evan expected. A red-haired woman in a tailored pantsuit sat next to a man who took his fashion cues from David Bowie and Billie Porter.

"Evan Malone, meet Jenna Anderson and Adrian Harris." Joe made room for Evan to sit beside him. "Evan's a hunter, going after Willis Osborn. Jenna and Adrian are friends. They'll be helpful in finding Seth."

"Which one is the witch?" Evan asked, trying to imagine either of the people sitting across from him in that role.

"Neither. That would be me," the bartender said as he wandered over.

"Evan, this is Johnny Laveccia. He owns the place."

"You can speak candidly here. I've made sure no one else can hear you," Johnny said with a smirk.

"Pleased to meet all of you," Evan replied. "Now, how do we stop Osborn and save Seth?"

"There's no 'we,'" Jenna said. "You tell us what's going on, and the professionals take it from here."

"Fuck that." Evan stood, and Joe yanked him back to the seat. "Look, I don't know who you are—"

"Supernatural Secret Service," she replied without missing a beat.

Evan glanced at Joe. "Is that a real thing?"

Joe nodded. "Afraid so."

Jenna shot Joe a deadly glance. "Not helping."

"Chill," Adrian said. "I want to hear him out."

Evan figured that Jenna and Adrian were in their mid-thirties. He knew they looked at him and couldn't see past his age. Seth had a way of commanding respect despite his relative youth, but he wasn't here, and if Evan didn't pull off a rescue, Seth was never coming back.

He straightened his back and squared his shoulders. "Willis Osborn was a member of a coven devoted to Rhyfel Gremory, a dark warlock who died one hundred years ago. When a sheriff and his posse killed the warlock, the coven scattered and swore vengeance on the descendants of the lawmen. One of those witches killed Seth's brother Jesse, and Seth vowed he'd wipe them all out. I'm also a descendant of one of the deputies, and Seth saved my life.

"We've dealt with four members of the coven so far—permanently. Seth and I came to Cleveland to stop the fifth, but Osborn figured out we were coming, and he's been trying to get to us first. He grabbed Seth. The next descendant here in Cleveland is a cop who thinks we're the bad guys. I could sure use some help going after Osborn, but with or without you, I'm going to save my partner." Evan waited to see their reaction.

"He's got spirit," Adrian said, with a glance toward Joe. Adrian wore an immaculate white suit over a dark blue silk shirt. An expensive watch graced one wrist. The large diamond stud in his ear looked real. Evan wondered if Adrian was an actor or musician. He carried himself like someone used to being in the spotlight.

"You've come mighty close to admitting to a string of felonies," Jenna advised.

"I never liked Osborn," Johnny remarked with a bored expression.

Joe rolled his eyes. "Jenna—lighten up. Adrian—don't toy with someone who's got nothing left to lose. Johnny, pay attention. I asked you to meet Evan because you've got a common foe—Osborn."

Evan stared at Jenna and Adrian. "You're descendants too?"

Joe shook his head. "No. But Jenna's people have been watching Osborn closely for a while on all kinds of interesting possible charges." He gave Jenna a look, and she reluctantly nodded.

"Osborn started out as an apothecary, and once he gained quasi-immortality, he expanded his pharmacy," she said. "Started compounding drugs for supernatural creatures' metabolisms. When his customers are strung out, they're even more dangerous. Osborn's a user himself, augmented with magic. Lately, his cronies added a take-out food menu to their options."

Evan felt sick to his stomach. "People?"

She nodded. "They grab ride-share fares, and before the person knows what's going on, they're delivered to an address where they're the guest of honor for dinner—as the entree."

"So, if you had all this on him, why is he still free?" Evan challenged.

Jenna met his gaze. "Knowing something and being able to prove it in court are two different things—especially when most people don't believe anything paranormal is real. Not to mention the crooked cops and judges Osborn has in his pocket. We can petition to try him before a Tribunal, a special court for supernatural creatures and crimes, but that's a complex process."

"And you didn't know he's been killing people for a century from the deputies' families?"

"Believe it or not—no," Jenna replied, looking a little embarrassed. "No one dug up the connections—no pun intended—between one cycle of murders and the next."

"How about you show us what you've got so far, and we can figure out where to go from there," Joe said, clearly trying to stave off a fight.

Evan took a deep breath to get hold of his temper and nodded. "Once the witch disciples realized Seth and I were on their trail, they sped up their rituals, taking their victims early to power up. They're most vulnerable in the middle of the ritual, but that doesn't leave any margin for error."

"We've had friends helping us scour records for Osborn's aliases, assets, addresses, holding companies, and associates," Evan continued. "Including his Darke Web activity. We didn't come into this blind."

"Friends?" Jenna asked.

"They fought the last witch disciple in Charleston—with Sorren and his allies," Joe said with a tone of warning in his voice. Jenna's eyebrows rose, and Evan thought he saw a glint of new respect in her eyes.

"Okay," she said, drawing out the syllables. "You're just full of surprises."

Adrian looked amused.

Evan walked them through the information Teag and Travis had supplied, as well as what he and Seth put together and the latest notes from the library.

"We're pretty sure we know where the anchor is, and we've got friends with extra abilities working on deciphering the inscription so we can open the vault. To stop Osborn, we'll need to destroy his anchor, take his amulet, and prevent or interrupt his ritual. Since he's a powerful witch, that's even harder than it sounds."

"How did you do it before?" Adrian looked sincerely interested.

"Skin of our teeth," Evan replied. "Seth and I both nearly died escaping the disciple in Richmond. We had help from Travis and Brent for the Pittsburgh warlock."

"Travis Dominick?" Jenna asked, surprised again. "You do run with an interesting crowd."

"Seth's mentors helped out in Boone. And as Joe said, Sorren's friends worked with us in Charleston. Which is why I'd like to have your help, but one way or another, I'm going after Seth," Evan said, bracing for an argument.

Joe looked at Johnny. "How much grief will the Cleveland covens give you over causing Osborn trouble?"

Johnny shook his head. "Trouble? Maybe applause. They fear him, but no one likes him. Especially after his 'business partner' in St. Louis got killed."

"That was another one of the witch disciples and Osborn's brother," Evan replied.

Jenna's eyebrow rose, but she continued. "Their partnership went way back—farther than good record-keeping. Whatever went wrong not only killed Osborn's brother, but it took out most of the brother's organization. We did the clean-up afterward—there's nothing left."

"Saves Seth and me a road trip," Evan muttered. He looked to Johnny. "Do the covens know what happened, or are they just assuming the worst?"

"Not sure. Assuming the worst about Osborn is usually a wise choice. Something you must keep in mind is that Osborn's supernatural drug ring goes beyond him personally," Johnny warned. "There is a cartel that moves the drugs to users all over the country, maybe the world. They won't like having their supplier removed."

"Mob ties?" Jenna asked.

Johnny glared at her. "I wouldn't know. But I suspect no *legitimate* business organization would deal with them."

Great, Evan thought. *It's not just Osborn. He's got a whole fuckin' monster Mafia working for him.* "I guess that explains the goons and the hitmen."

Jenna looked at him with a cool, appraising expression. Adrian grinned, seeming to enjoy her surprise.

"We need a plan, fast," Evan reminded them. "We've only got a couple of days until the full moon. Osborn can kill Seth for a battery-boost without needing to 'harvest' Derek Nelson early and lose out on a bigger power-up later on."

Johnny stared at Evan with a thoughtful expression. "I don't dispute that Seth is in great danger as Osborn's prisoner or that Osborn would see removing Seth—and you—as a way to protect himself. But I wonder if there's something else involved."

"Like what?" Evan challenged.

"Osborn touts his drugs with a personal testimonial about how he was badly injured and then fully recovered with the help of his potions," Johnny said. "But there have been rumors that his recovery wasn't as complete as he would like others to believe. Talk on the street is that the 'medicines' are addictive—which would suggest that Osborn might be his own biggest customer. He might try to use magical means to sustain himself."

"Which would be a reason to speed up the sacrifices—and do some extra," Evan replied.

"Perhaps. I will make some discreet inquiries among the covens and other…associates…to see what's being said," Johnny said.

"I'll have my team check the list of properties you came up with against the ones we're already watching. If there's been an uptick in activity, it might help us figure out what Osborn's planning," Jenna said.

Adrian leaned forward with a cat-that-ate-the-canary smile. "My family's software company specializes in data mining. It's especially good at finding obscure connections. Text me a list of names, and I'll tell you more about them than they know themselves."

"Deal." Evan sent him the list of names.

"As luck would have it," Adrian continued, "I'm attending a fundraiser tomorrow night for a charity Osborn likes to support. Good PR and all. He may be there. How about you go with me and see if that stirs up the hornet's nest? The last time I saw him at a benefit dinner, he didn't look well. If he's had a sudden change of health, that could mean he's drawing on extra power."

"I don't have anything that would be suitable to wear."

Adrian gave him the once-over, making Evan feel like he'd been scanned with X-ray vision. "I'll get you what you need. I think this could be important."

"Thank you," Evan replied. "I appreciate any help you can give me. I need to find Seth—and soon."

He left with assurances from his new allies that he would hear from them quickly. Joe lingered to talk with Johnny, while Adrian and Jenna went their separate ways. When Evan returned to his truck, he found Officer Nelson loitering nearby.

"Is there a problem, Officer?" Evan asked, although he was certain Nelson had no real reason to bother him.

"You're still here. That's enough of a problem."

Evan wasn't in the mood to trade barbs. "What's your point?"

"Just letting you know that we've got eyes on you," Nelson replied. "When you make trouble, we'll be there. Better stay on the straight and narrow, or you'll be on your way out of town before you know what hit you. Or maybe you should just leave now."

"I'll keep that in mind," Evan said. "If I'm free to go—"

Nelson gave a sarcastic salute. "I'll be seeing you."

Evan climbed into the truck and let out a long breath. *Am I bad for being disappointed that Osborn didn't take Nelson instead of Seth?*

In the past, Evan sympathized with the witch disciple's intended victims. After all, he'd been one of them. Everyone else they had saved allied with them, even if they were initially skeptical. Nelson was the first to be manipulated by the disciple into opposing them.

That's going to make saving him a lot harder.

Evan drove, alert for anyone following him. He didn't spot a tail, so after a few more turns and switchbacks, he headed for the campground and tried to ignore his restlessness.

Today felt like a complete failure. While he had gained information and allies, he still lacked a plan to rescue Seth. Despite everyone believing it was unlikely for Osborn to sacrifice Seth before the full moon, Evan didn't like risking his lover's life on a bet.

Evan hadn't been hungry since Seth was taken, but he knew he needed to eat to keep up his strength for the fight, even if everything tasted like ash. Once he was back at the RV, he put a frozen pizza in the oven.

While dinner baked, Evan set up his laptop on the kitchen table. Two emails topped his list. One from Travis Dominick—and the other from Parker.

Evan picked Travis's first.

Evan—Brent made an interesting discovery. Over the last year, twelve members of the extended families of the deputies' descendants in both Cleveland and St. Louis have gone missing. No bodies have been found, and authorities haven't declared foul play, although the families are pushing for better investigations.

This is unlikely to be a coincidence. My theory is that the warlock is addicted to getting the 'hit' from Gremory's energy, and he might even be skimming from the power that keeps Gremory trapped. If he gets a big level up from killing a direct descendant, then he may have found a way to leech energy from less direct family members without killing them quickly. The good news is that he'd have a reason to keep them alive longer.

Be extra careful. If Osborn has done his homework—and Brent and I suspect he has—then he knows you're a descendant as well. You're at risk.

The email ended with a promise to help however possible and an invitation to call any time.

Evan put his elbows on the table and held his head in his hands. *Seth and I were supposed to be fighting the witch disciple together. How did it get this crazy?*

He took the pizza out of the oven and waited for it to cool. In the meantime, he checked Parker's email.

Let's not fight about Dad. I'd like to see you. I'm in Columbus, Ohio. I'll drive to wherever you are.

It would be good for me to get out of town for a little while. I've had the feeling I was being followed, and there's a strange guy I've spotted in several places—I think he's tailing me. Don't know why, but it creeps me out. I'd feel safer closer to you.

Shit, Evan thought. *Parker isn't the eldest, so he wasn't the disciple's target, but he's still a descendant. What if Osborn found him?*

Evan took the warning to his marrow. He resolved to discuss the situation with Joe tomorrow.

Evan considered his words carefully and began to type. *I'm in East Cleveland temporarily, not far from Forest Hill Park,* he wrote. *If you come to town, we can get together. Just be careful—there have been some carjack-ings lately.* The hold-ups were a fiction to justify the warning, but since Travis had suggested that the disciple could make use of the other descendants, Evan wasn't taking any chances. *We need to talk—and I'll do my best to listen. Please come.*

Evan thought he might have to wait until morning for a reply. But apparently Parker was online because only minutes passed before he received an answer.

Thank you. I'll find a motel in Cleveland and let you know where I am. I'm looking forward to seeing you. I'll be there tomorrow.

EVAN KNEW SLEEP WOULDN'T COME EASY, SO HE MADE ANOTHER POT OF coffee and spread out his papers on the table, with his laptop in the corner. He pulled up a map of downtown in a program meant to set up walking tour destinations and started to plug in the addresses of Osborn's properties, past and present. He added the library where Seth had gone missing, the observatory, and the entrance to the abandoned subway station Seth had been about to text to him.

When Evan was done, he made the map as big as possible and

stared at the location markers, looking for a clue about where to search for Seth.

The Osborn-owned building closest to the library was the head-quarters for the pharmaceutical company. *I doubt they carried an unconscious man in through the lobby, and it's not a factory, so there's no loading dock.*

Some of the old addresses were now vacant lots. Evan removed those markers on the map after checking to ensure there were no underground tunnels beneath the land. The manufacturing operation was in a light industry section of the city, and Evan didn't see an advantage for Osborn to have Seth stashed there.

Many of the other buildings were old warehouses. One listing caught his eye—the same one Seth had flagged in his library notes. The physical rehabilitation facility once belonged to the local Catholic hospital system. Five years ago, the rehab facility was de-licensed and shuttered. Osborn bought the property, but as far as Evan could tell, never did anything with it. And the property was right next to the defunct subway station.

The hospital would be a perfect place to stash prisoners—Seth and the other descendants' family members who've gone missing. The subway tunnel would work for his rituals. He drew a circle around that site, intending to have a closer look.

Evan walked back to the kitchen and poured himself some whiskey. The RV seemed too empty and quiet without Seth. He went into the bedroom and pulled one of Seth's flannel shirts out of the dirty laundry, taking in the smell of sweat, soap, and shampoo before slipping it on and pulling it close around him.

For the rest of the evening, Evan dove deep on the internet looking for satellite photos of the area around Osborn's buildings and floor plans of the old rehab center. Information on the old subway tunnels was harder to find than he expected.

Evan decided that once daylight came, he'd go down to the historical association's office and see who he could sweet talk into telling him more. Maybe they'd even have blueprints or photos that would help him narrow down where Osborn might do his rituals.

When he was finally groggy, and the whiskey numbed his heart,

Evan checked the locks and wardings, turned off lights, and headed to the bedroom, almost too tired to take off his clothing. He slept on Seth's side of the bed, hungry for his scent, needing to feel their connection.

Where are you, Seth? Please don't be dead. I need you here with me. I'm coming for you. Hang on.

~

A FEW HOURS LATER, EVAN WOKE WITH THE TASTE OF STALE WHISKEY IN HIS mouth and the dregs of bad dreams haunting his memory. His phone buzzed, and he reached for it, half-awake.

"Have you eaten yet?" Parker asked, sounding far too chipper. "I got in late last night. I thought maybe we could have breakfast. If you're not tied up, I'd like to spend as much of the day together as we can. We've got a lot to catch up on."

Groggily, Evan realized that it was Saturday, and Parker's assumption that he was free wasn't far-fetched. Parker had not only made the first move to call; he'd driven in from Columbus to see him. They might be emotionally distanced, but they were brothers.

Still, Seth's life was in danger, and Evan couldn't rely on anyone else to save him. The clock was ticking. Parker's arrival was incredibly bad timing.

"Breakfast is a great idea. Then I've got some errands to run, but you're welcome to come with me if that won't bore you to tears," Evan offered, hoping he was doing the right thing.

"I don't mind tagging along. There's plenty to talk about."

Evan suggested a diner he'd passed that was close to the historical association, and Parker agreed to meet him there in forty-five minutes That gave Evan time to get a shower and have some coffee and let Parker navigate unfamiliar Cleveland traffic.

He walked into the diner ten minutes early and scanned the people sitting in the booths, wondering if he would even recognize Parker after all this time.

Evan looked past the lanky young man sprawled in the rear corner booth before his gaze shifted back, caught by something familiar about the man's eyes. Parker looked up then and nodded in recognition. *Maybe I didn't change as much as he did.*

Evan felt awkward and on edge. He and Parker had been very close —everyone joked about them being "twins" despite the age difference. Now, he found himself looking at a stranger with a vaguely familiar face and wondering if they could ever bridge the lost time.

Parker rose when Evan approached. He held out his hand, and Evan shook it, then went along willingly when Parker pulled him into a quick hug.

"Good to see you," Parker said as they sat. "You don't look any different."

"You do," Evan admitted, sliding into the seat across from Parker. "All grown up."

They ordered quickly when the server came. Coffee for both. Pancakes and bacon for Parker, a waffle and sausage for Evan. After she walked away, they sat in uncomfortable silence for a moment.

"So…college?" Evan asked, remembering that Parker had been taking classes the last time they had talked.

Parker nodded. "Yeah—I'm working on an engineering degree as I get enough to pay for the classes. In Columbus—I had to get out of Oklahoma." He paused. "How about you?

"I did a lot of bartending for a while, but I managed to get an associate's degree in graphic design, and now I have my own company, so I can work from anywhere. Still doing photography when I can." Evan felt a surge of pride that Parker had the initiative to escape and start on a degree.

"That's fantastic. I'm a clerk for a personnel company right now, and I have a couple of part-time gigs, but I'm still figuring out what I want to do for the long run after I finish college," Parker replied.

Their food arrived fast, providing a break from conversation. Evan made sure to keep an eye on the restaurant and its patrons, watching for anyone who might take too much notice of them.

By unspoken agreement, they didn't mention family. Parker told him about his most recent adventures, while Evan came up with stories about the funnier moments from his restaurant days.

When they made it through breakfast without anyone trying to kill them, Evan let out a sigh of relief. Parker insisted on picking up the check, and Evan promised to pay for lunch.

Once they walked outside, Parker hesitated. "We probably don't need two cars."

"How about if I follow you back to your hotel, and you leave your car there and ride with me?" Evan suggested. That left him in control and also meant they had the warded vehicle with the hidden cache of weapons.

Parker was fine with that, and fortunately his hotel was nearby. He gave a low whistle of approval when he climbed into the truck. "Nice wheels, man."

Evan felt a stab of sadness. "It's not mine. It belongs to Seth—my partner."

Parker cocked his head and gave him a look. "Partner in the business or—"

"Life partner. Boyfriend isn't serious enough."

Parker nodded. "So...where's Seth? Do I get to meet him?"

Evan looked away. "He's not around today. But I'd like to introduce you to him when I can." He was trying not to lie to Parker, and he didn't want to drag his brother into his mess. Evan felt acutely aware of how little he knew his brother after all this time. He decided he'd keep his secrets until he had a better idea of the stranger who sat next to him.

"How about you?" Evan asked, eager to change the subject. "Got a girl in Columbus?"

Parker shook his head. "No one special. I dated, but haven't found that certain someone yet."

Evan couldn't resist a fond smile. "I didn't think I'd find the right person, but Seth found me. We're good together. We haven't set a date but...I think he's it for me."

The reality of the situation hit him, making Evan catch his breath. *Please be okay. Hang on. I'm going to rescue you.*

"Marriage?" Parker sounded surprised.

"You do know we can do that now, right?" Evan didn't know whether to be amused or offended.

"Yeah. Just surprised," Parker said. "I didn't mean anything by it.

I've realized that most of what people told me wasn't right. Now that I've left, I've got a lot to learn."

Evan nodded, still not trusting himself to speak. He knew what the church and community—and their parents—believed. Of course, that colored Parker's views. *Hell, it screwed up my head about myself until I worked through it.*

"Thank you for being willing to re-think what you were taught," Evan said.

"Thanks for giving me the chance," Parker replied.

Evan wove through traffic, checking the mirror often to assure himself they weren't being followed.

"Do they do a lot of speed traps around here? You seem to be watching your rear view a lot," Parker asked.

"That's what I've heard. Don't want to get a ticket."

When they got to the historical association, Evan turned to Parker. "I need to look for some old floor plans and blueprints for a project I'm working on. Not the most exciting stuff, but important." *It's the most important thing—saving Seth.*

"I learned a lot about research with some of my classes. Just let me know what to do, and I'll help," Parker said.

To Evan's relief, the archivist didn't object to his request and accepted his cover story about working on illustrations for a presentation. After giving them a quick tour to know where to look for materials, she left them on their own.

Evan threw himself into his work, and Parker proved to be a willing and clever helper. They didn't speak much except to retrieve one resource after another, and with his brother's assistance, Evan got through much more than he could have alone. By the time they left, he not only had the blueprints for the rehab hospital, but he had detailed maps of the old subway, plus schematics and engineering specs.

"You're going to have a very thorough presentation," Parker said as they cleaned up after themselves.

"It's a high-stakes kind of thing. Once in a lifetime chance," Evan replied, knowing that he was skating on the edge of the truth.

Evan stopped at the archivist's desk on the way out. "Thank you for helping us."

"Did you find everything you needed?" She leaned forward and waved them toward her with a conspiratorial expression. "You might want to go out the staff door. There were two rough-looking men hanging around the front when I came back from my break. They didn't bother me, but maybe they didn't think I was worth the effort. It could be different for you."

"Thank you," Evan said, sure they didn't want to tangle with the strangers. "You've been very kind."

Evan bustled Parker toward the side door. "What's going on? Why are you worried?" Parker pressed.

"I ran into some trouble with a couple of locals," Evan said. "I guess they recognized the truck and decided to make problems for me."

"Do you owe them money?"

Evan stared at him. "What? No! But they aren't much for talking, and I don't want either of us to get hurt. Just move quickly and be quiet—it's not far to the truck."

He eased the side door open and looked both ways. Going left was the shorter route, but they might be seen by the goons at the front. Turning right meant walking around the block, but he figured that the slight bit of extra time was worth the safety.

"Follow me," Evan said, heading off at a fast pace.

"Why are we in a hurry? Evan, what's going on?"

Voices rose behind them, and when Evan glanced over his shoulder, he saw two muscular men hurrying toward them. The truck was in sight but not close enough.

"Run!" Evan ordered. He used the key fob and heard the beep that let him know the truck was unlocked and tossed the keys to Parker. "Get in the truck. Don't let in anyone but me. Even if they grab me. I'll explain later. Just go." He shoved Parker, sending him on his way.

Evan didn't want a fight, but the goons would be on them before he and Parker could get to the truck, and he needed to protect his brother. Parker had no part in Evan's problem with the witch disciple except to be born into a cursed family. Evan wanted to send him home safely, none the wiser.

He heard the truck door slam and braced himself for a fight. *Maybe I can slow them down and still get away.*

"Someone wants to talk to you," one of the men growled, a big guy who looked like he should be a bouncer at a rough bar.

"We've got something you want," the other taunted. "Don't you want to see if it's as pretty as when you lost it?"

Evan's heart thudded, but he stood his ground and silently began the rote fire spell. He stretched out one hand and called the magic, sending a shaft of flame toward his pursuers.

The two goons threw themselves out of the way of the fire, and behind Evan, the truck's horn blared and its lights flashed on and off. He heard the crunch of tires, and a glance over his shoulder told him that Parker was behind the wheel, bearing down on them.

The high beams flared, blinding his pursuers.

"Get in!" Parker yelled, and Evan scrambled for the passenger door. Once he was inside with the doors locked, Parker revved the engine, a clear threat to the men who pursued them. Evan chuckled as they fled.

"Thanks," Evan said as his pursuers disappeared down the alley.

Parker backed up to the street and then turned toward the hotel. "Who were those guys? Why were they after you?"

Evan didn't answer right away, but he realized he couldn't hold off Parker's questions forever.

"They've seen that you're with me. You aren't safe alone. Let's stop at your hotel to get your things, and then you can come home with me. I'll tell you what I can."

"You're in danger."

Evan nodded. "Seth's been kidnapped. I can't trust the police. I have friends helping me, but we're going to have to rescue Seth ourselves. It won't be easy. You shouldn't be anywhere near here when that happens."

"Who kidnapped him?"

"The man who killed his brother."

Parker stared at him. "What have you gotten yourself into?"

Evan sighed. "It's a long story. You wouldn't believe me if I tried to tell you."

"I saw you throw fire at those men, and I didn't run away. That should count for something," Parker challenged.

"You saw that?" Evan thought his body blocked the view.

"So, you're a gay witch?"

Despite the situation, Evan laughed. "That's the least of our worries."

"I can see why you don't want to go home—although you'd be totally safe. With as much hairspray as the old ladies there use, you could light up the whole town with one fire-bolt."

"That wouldn't make them want me around," Evan countered.

"Maybe not—but they'd be a whole lot nicer to your face."

They laughed at that, as inappropriate as it was. Before long, Parker pulled up at the hotel. "I don't have much to grab—I didn't have time to unpack. Are you coming in?"

Evan shook his head. "No. I'll stand guard here. Be fast."

He thought maybe his brother would change his mind once he was out of the truck, but Parker was back in five minutes with a duffel bag and a computer backpack.

"Figured I'd travel light since I wasn't sure if you were going to send me home as soon as I got here," Parker confessed.

Since Evan had strongly considered doing that, he just nodded. "How long do you have the room for?"

"The weekend. I was optimistic."

Evan chuckled. "Good. We'll come back for your car tomorrow."

Parker glanced at him in surprise when Evan pulled into the campground. "That's where you're staying?" he asked when Evan parked in front of the camper.

"Seth and I live in the RV; makes it easy to move around," Evan replied. He made sure to park where Seth had warded a space and led Parker to the trailer. He held his breath until Parker was past the protections, still afraid that his brother's sudden appearance might not be as coincidental as it seemed and that the wardings would refuse him entry.

Evan reached beneath his shirt and pulled out the two protective silver medallions he never left home without. He removed one, which he handed to Parker.

"Wear this. It will help keep you safe."

Parker accepted the necklace skeptically. "From what?"

"Dark magic and infernal creatures who dislike silver." Evan sighed. "Just…trust me on this, please."

Parker dropped the chain around his neck and tucked the medallion into his shirt with a shy smile. "Thanks. I feel safer already." His teasing tone told Evan that Parker would follow his lead, even if he didn't completely understand. That warmed a part of Evan's big brother heart that had gone dormant for too long.

"This is very nice," Parker said, looking around. Evan sometimes forgot his first reaction to an RV with leather couches, an electric fireplace, bump-outs for more space, a well-appointed kitchen, and a surprising amount of elbow room.

"Seth's parents bought the RV and the truck for their retirement traveling. Then they were killed in a car accident not long after Seth's brother was murdered. The house burned in a mysterious fire. All Seth had left was his motorcycle, the truck, and the fifth wheeler."

Parker stared at Evan in shock. "Seriously? I think you'd better back the fuck up and start from the beginning."

Evan nodded. "Have a seat. I'm going to make coffee. Then I'll tell you as much as I can."

Parker made a slow circle around the living room, taking in the photographs of Seth and Evan and the homey touches that were a mix of items the two of them had collected in their travels and things Seth's mom had bought.

Evan brought over two hot mugs of coffee and set one down in front of Parker before taking a seat across from him. "Do you remember when Uncle Vince died suddenly thirteen years ago?"

"Dad's older brother?" Parker asked before taking a sip of his drink. "Yeah."

Evan nodded. "And you've heard Dad talk about how his father's older brother also died young."

"You think they're connected?"

"I know they are. Because I would have been the next to die last Halloween if Seth hadn't saved me." Evan told Parker the whole story about defeating the first witch disciple and Evan's near miss.

"For a hundred years, the warlocks sacrificed the descendants of the deputies who executed their master. It wasn't just our uncle and great-uncle—it was the oldest of each generation back to the turn of the last century," Evan continued.

"And you and Seth travel around fighting evil, like those guys on TV?"

"It's scarier when it's real," Evan replied. "Blood doesn't wash out of clothing well, and our hair never looks that good in a fight."

"I'm serious," Parker complained.

"So am I. This is the fifth witch disciple, and because of him, the sixth is dead. That still leaves six more to go," Evan said.

"Why is this your responsibility?" Parker protested. "Aren't there people who get paid to handle these sorts of things?"

"Secret government organizations and Vatican groups do some of the work. But a lot of monsters exist, and there aren't enough people who fight them," Evan replied. "No one realized the pattern with Gremory's disciples for a century—all those deaths—before Seth picked up on it. How many more people would have died? Me, for one."

Parker shivered. "Don't say things like that."

"It's true."

"So why did they take Seth?"

"Seth's still a descendant. Any of the witches could power up by killing him—or me. And while it wouldn't do them as much good, you are also in danger."

"But you and Seth got rid of the witch who tried to kill you."

"The witch disciples each chose a family to follow, which kept it organized so they weren't all fighting over the same descendant," Evan replied. "But any of us would work as a sacrifice."

"And the warlock here took Seth? Then how do you know—"

"I don't," Evan said, raising his head defiantly, unwilling to have Parker speak his greatest fear aloud. "But the ritual would be strongest at the full moon, so I think he'll wait until then if it's his intention to do the magic. There may be other spells he can work with descendants without killing them. Several others have gone missing recently."

"Do you know how crazy this sounds? Witches, warlocks, spells, rituals—it's like our old pastor who said everyone who plays role-playing games is worshiping Satan." Parker rose and started to pace, sounding a little freaked out.

"No games, and Satan's not involved," Evan replied. "Just evil men who use their magic and wealth to hurt others."

"And those men who chased us?"

"Pretty sure they work for Osborn—the disciple. I didn't want to wait around to ask them. But now that they've linked you with me, they'll figure out who you are, and you'll be a target. If you weren't already," Evan said. "You might be safe if you hightail it back to Oklahoma, but not if you stay in Ohio. I'm sorry you got dragged into this."

"Dad would have a fit if he heard you."

"Dad knew."

Parker's eyes went wide. "What do you mean? How do you know?"

"Why did Dad move the family to Oklahoma when we were in Richmond for generations? He and Mom hate Oklahoma. He's never liked his job. So why did we go there? Why did we stay? He left Richmond to outrun the witch disciple," Evan said. "He was so worried about his son being 'gay,' he forgot to mention that bit of family history. So, guess where I drifted back to? Richmond."

Parker's hands shook, and his coffee sloshed when he set down his cup. "Damn. I wish I could argue, but what you're saying makes a lot of sense."

"Maybe you don't remember before we left Richmond, but Mom and Dad weren't religious then. I don't remember going to church when we were young, let alone going multiple times a week. Then Uncle Vince died, and we moved and got religion."

"You think it was because he was trying to protect you, even if he didn't know from what?"

Evan shrugged. "Guess he forgot all about that when he found out I was gay."

Parker looked chagrined. "What a clusterfuck. I'm sorry, Evan. For not standing up for you back then."

"You were just a kid." Evan paused. "Dad's really that sick?"

Parker nodded. "So Mom says. She wasn't happy when I moved

away, so it could be an exaggeration, but I do think there's something actually wrong."

"Are you going back?" Evan asked.

"There's nothing I can do to help if I go," Parker said. "Jim's there, and no, he hasn't changed a bit. He sounds just like Dad. And Mom's got her friends and the church. Hell, people probably have a casserole sign-up and prayer chain going. If I stay here, I can help you find Seth."

"Why would you do that?" Evan stared at Parker, baffled.

"Because you're my brother. And I missed you."

Parker's answer caught Evan off guard. "Thank you," he said after a moment. "Just realize that Seth and I have both trained for this fight. We've gained skills—like the magic you saw. I appreciate your willingness, but I won't put you in danger."

"About that," Parker said. "I'm not useless—and I'm not a kid anymore. I'm good at research—and I have my computer. I can watch a video feed or relay information. Run the comm links." He brightened. "I've always wanted to do that."

"It could come in handy," Evan admitted. "If you want to stay, I could use the help."

"At the very least, I can make coffee and cook dinner. An army moves on its stomach, after all." Parker grinned.

Evan checked his messages. Joe said that Johnny was touching base with the other covens but didn't have answers yet, and he hadn't heard back from Jenna. Travis Dominick and Teag Logan did have news on the observatory inscription, and their answers matched, leaving Evan feeling confident that at least part of their plan was going right.

"What's next?" Parker asked.

"My friend Joe is recruiting reinforcements for us to go after Seth," Evan said. "I think I know where he's being kept. Just in case Osborn is still planning to do the ritual at the full moon, I need to break into the abandoned observatory and steal his anchor—he needs that to work the magic. Friends just worked out the code so I can open the safe."

"Okay. When do we go?"

Evan stared at Parker. "It's dangerous. And technically, it's against the law. We'll be breaking and entering."

Parker sniffed. "Please. Not my first time. Don't you remember Old Man Anderson's farm back home? I engineered senior skip day and got us past guard dogs, an electric fence, and a bad-tempered bull named Floyd."

"I'm not saying you don't have talent," Evan replied with a heavy dose of sarcasm. "But this involves magic and the police."

"I can't do magic, so let me give the cops a merry chase. Don't spread it around, but I've outrun the cops more than a few times when keggers got busted."

"Shocking," Evan said, deadpan.

"I'm practically a criminal," Parker said in a conspiratorial whisper, reminding Evan why he had missed his brother so much. The two of them had always been on the same wavelength.

Evan weighed his options. Sitting around while Seth was missing was driving him nuts. Retrieving the anchor might slow Osborn down, and it gave them a valuable piece of leverage, as well as the means to stop the sacrifice ritual. Joe and his friends were busy hunting down other essential information through their contacts. And Evan knew he shouldn't go to the observatory alone.

"All right, you're in," he said, although he couldn't quash his reservations. "We'll go tomorrow, right after we bring your car to the campground. Make sure you wear your running shoes because you might need them."

"YOU'RE GOING TO A PARTY?" PARKER ASKED, AS EVAN ADJUSTED THE TUX Adrian had delivered to the campground office.

"Fundraiser—and the main suspect for Seth's kidnapping is going to be there," Evan replied. "I'll be with someone Osborn doesn't dare touch. Pretty sure Joe and Jenna will be there undercover as well. I need to get a feel for this guy—and I'll do my best not to throttle him on sight."

"What do you want me to do while you're gone?" Parker asked.

"Stay inside the RV and don't open the door." Evan fussed with his cummerbund. "We've got plenty of DVDs and good Wi-Fi, so you can kick back and relax. There's soda in the fridge and pizza in the freezer. Just don't go anywhere and don't tell anyone where we're located."

"I can do that," Parker said. "This is a pretty comfy place."

Evan smiled wistfully. "Most of that is Seth. He's really made it a home for us." He put on his tux jacket, and Parker nodded in approval.

"Look at you—Jackson Evan Malone, secret agent man," Parker teased

"Not bad, considering I never made it to senior prom." He heard the rumble of a car outside and glanced out the window. "Figures Adrian drives a Maserati."

"Holy fuck," Parker said, looking out the window and letting out a low whistle. "You're going in style."

"Let's just hope we pick up some useful information," he told Parker. "We need to get Seth away from Osborn and safely home."

"Just remember—'shaken, not stirred,'" Parker said, clapping Evan on the shoulder on his way out of the door. "You're Malone—Jackson Evan Malone. Gotta play the part."

"Dork. You know I hate 'Jackson.'" Evan smiled from the ribbing despite his worries.

"Eh, says the uber-dweeb," Parker countered with a smirk. "Knock 'em dead."

Evan had butterflies in his stomach as he walked out to the sports car. Part of him felt guilty for attending a plush event while Seth was imprisoned, even if it was to help find a way to save him. Although he knew that attending the fundraiser with Adrian was completely platonic, Evan also felt weirdly unfaithful.

"What should I expect?" Evan asked as Adrian pulled out into traffic. "Nice car, by the way."

"Thanks," Adrian replied with a grin. "Bonus—if anyone chases us, we can outrun them all."

"Hoping that doesn't happen, but good to know."

Adrian sobered. "I've been helping Jenna and Joe keep tabs on Osborn for a while. This organization is a charity—not something he funnels money from. Believe me, I checked. Totally up-and-up. Of course, that's how he maintains his 'good guy' reputation, kissing puppies and petting babies."

"I think it's the other way around," Evan snarked at Adrian's intentional mistake.

"Really? I don't have a lot of experience with either one," Adrian replied.

Despite his nerves, Evan found himself becoming more comfortable with his new companion.

"Couple of things you need to know," Adrian said, growing serious. "The charity is legit—but a lot of the donors aren't what they appear to be. Remember how Osborn's pharmaceutical company caters to supernatural creatures? Well, some of them will be in attendance. They're theoretically upstanding entrepreneurs. Some of them are also vampires, shifters, werewolves, and other creatures."

"Witches?"

Adrian shook his head. "Unlikely. The other covens might not oppose Osborn outright, but they fear and dislike him. They won't offer to help him unless he holds their feet to the fire. Johnny's willingness to take a stand is backed up by a major Mob family. And he's an exception because he's got a history with Joe. It's all a bit fraught."

Evan frowned. "How do you rate going to a shindig for supernatural creatures when you're human?"

"Am I?" Adrian's mischievous smile was mesmerizing. Then as quickly as the charisma came, it vanished.

Fae? Evan wondered. If Joe trusted Adrian, then Evan told himself he was safe, but he felt rattled by the reveal.

"You've got some magic yourself," Adrian said, skating past any further discussion of his abilities. "I can smell it on you."

"I swear I took a shower," Evan joked, feeling a little off-kilter that Adrian noticed his abilities.

"Don't worry—they won't all be able to tell," Adrian reassured him. "Although Osborn may suspect if he's sent witches against you."

"I think that's the only way they got the drop on Seth," Evan confided. "He's an excellent fighter."

"Very possible. Which means that's how Osborn's likely to come after you," Adrian said. "You won't be the only human in the room.

But you are likely to be the only one who knows that most of the others aren't."

They aren't allowed to eat me, are they?

Adrian chuckled, as if he could guess Evan's thoughts. "Don't worry—you're not on the menu. Bad for donations. As far as his company goes, Osborn has plenty of human collaborators who don't care who uses his drugs as long as they get a return on their investment."

"What are we looking for?" Evan felt twitchy.

"Good question. Anything that doesn't fit," Adrian replied. "Take note of the people, especially the ones Osborn pays attention to. Notice who's trying to suck up to him. See who he ignores. It's like watching a whole constellation in orbit around him and trying to figure out the push and pull."

"He hasn't bothered to come after us himself," Evan said. "Coward."

Adrian frowned. "That might be to your advantage. If he underestimates you, he won't bring out the big guns until it's too late."

They pulled up in front of the Cleveland Museum of Art. The featured charity worked with the museum to provide art programs for disadvantaged children, the kind of outreach no one could find objectionable.

Paparazzi were already waiting, and Evan winced at the unfamiliar glare of camera flashes as he and Adrian stepped out of the car. Adrian ignored the questions reporters yelled at him, and Evan was careful to stay in step while maintaining enough distance to allay speculation about them being a couple.

High-profile fancy events weren't part of the hunting life. But when he first moved to Richmond, Evan had been a server at some extravagant weddings and parties to pick up extra cash. He'd seen a different side of life than what he'd experienced and paid close attention in case he ever needed to mingle.

I guess it's true that no experience is ever wasted, Evan thought as he and Adrian walked the chasm between the reporters and photographers. Adrian swept along like he didn't even notice them, and Evan did his best to mimic his host's ennui.

Inside, the main gallery shimmered with white fairy lights. Ice sculptures glowed on the hors d'oeuvres tables, lit from within. A line had already formed at the bar, and Evan wished he dared to take the edge off his nerves, but he knew he needed to have his wits about him with Osborn nearby.

"Stick close," Adrian said as if Evan needed reminding. He seemed to know everyone, laughing and chatting with those around them in line at the bar, turning that mega-wattage charm up to the max. Evan scanned the crowd, looking for Osborn.

There he is. Evan spotted the witch disciple from the photographs. Willis Osborn was a thin man who dressed like a funeral director, with a long face, sharp features, and wire-rimmed glasses. He arrived without fanfare, but a frisson of excitement ran through the crowd at his entry, and well-wishers mobbed him like he was a rock star.

"Stay cool," Adrian murmured. "Stick to the plan. Joe and Jenna are servers. They're in the back. No, don't look. Just follow my lead. I want him to see you. We'll learn a lot from his reaction."

Evan tried hard not to fidget. Adrian ordered a gin martini, but Evan stuck to club soda with lime juice. After they got their drinks, Adrian drifted toward the hors d'oeuvres table, which was piled high with cold shrimp, roast beef mini-sliders, stuffed mushrooms, and a charcuterie spread.

He watched Osborn work the room. *Why did he take Seth? What has he done to him?* Evan tamped down his anger and struggled to keep his expression neutral.

Adrian positioned them where they would be visible, then let Osborn come to them.

"Adrian! So glad you could make it." Osborn approached them like an old friend, and Adrian shook his hand warmly.

"I wouldn't want to be anywhere else," Adrian replied, with a smile that Evan knew meant the opposite.

"And who is your friend?" Osborn's tone remained light, but Evan heard the shift when the witch disciple recognized him.

"Evan Malone," Adrian answered without missing a beat. "He's in town visiting."

"I've heard a lot about you," Evan said, keeping his voice level, with just a hint of a cold smile. He met Osborn's gaze and knew the other man took his meaning.

"How do you know Adrian?" Osborn asked.

"Oh, we go way back," Adrian answered before Evan could open his mouth. "Evan is the kind of friend you look out for," he added, sending a signal of his own.

Osborn hid his feelings well, but Evan saw the pull of displeasure at the corner of the man's mouth and how his lips thinned and eyes narrowed in anger.

Adrian's just declared me to be a protected species. If Osborn wants Adrian's money for his charity, he's going to need to tread carefully. If he's smart, he realizes that protection includes Seth as well.

"How lovely," Osborn said stiffly. He turned his attention back to Adrian. "I hope you've had a chance to look over the displays and read the materials that were sent out. The building renovation will help expand needed services, and if we meet funding goals, there'll also be two new staff positions added."

Osborn's voice had grown warm again now that he was in pitch mode. No doubt he hoped for a generous contribution from Adrian or his father's company. *Does he realize that—even aside from the people he's killed as a disciple—Adrian knows about the drugs for the supernatural set?*

Evan set down his empty glass, then took a stuffed mushroom and a flute of champagne from a passing server and studied Osborn closely. He looked haggard. His glasses didn't hide the dark shadows beneath his eyes, and his skin lacked a healthy glow. A gold ring with a large red stone was his only adornment. Evan wondered if it was true about Osborn being addicted to his own drugs and whether even magic was failing to counterbalance his old injury.

If he's stealing energy from Seth and the others who went missing, and he doesn't look any better than that, he must be in bad shape. Does that make him vulnerable?

Osborn and Adrian made small talk while Evan hung back and studied the room. He believed Adrian's warning that many of the attendees weren't fully human, but they did a good job of hiding in plain sight. Now that he looked for it, several of the guests had an unusual pallor, while others carried themselves with a predator's grace. Evan thought he spotted Joe and Jenna among the servers.

When he realized some of those people were looking back at him, Evan averted his gaze.

"The president of the foundation will be giving a short update at eight," Osborn was saying. "He promised to make it snappy. Of course, there are pledge cards by the door for those who can't stay. I do hope you'll enjoy the food."

With that, Osborn veered off to glad-hand more guests. Adrian fixed a plate from the buffet, but Evan's stomach was too tight to enjoy the food.

"I need to use the restroom," Evan excused himself, suddenly feeling like he wanted to throw up.

"Don't be gone long, or I'll have to come looking for you," Adrian said it half-jokingly, but Evan didn't put it past him.

The men's room was down the hallway outside the gallery. Since the museum was closed, the other areas were cordoned off, and with the lights turned down, it gave the huge building a spooky feel. Evan's footsteps echoed, and the people in the paintings he passed seemed to be watching him.

Evan kept his hand on the hex bag in his pocket, relieved to see no one else in the corridor. When he headed back to the main room, Osborn blocked his way. The smile on the witch disciple's face didn't reach his eyes.

"Adrian says you're new in town. You may find that Cleveland doesn't suit you," Osborn said in a pleasant voice. "It's an acquired taste. The city's quite dangerous if you aren't careful."

"I'll keep that in mind," Evan replied. "I hadn't actually planned to stay. My partner and I have unfinished business here."

"He may be finished with it before you are. Just something to consider." Osborn glided away into the thick of the partygoers before Evan could respond. He stood with his fists clenched, trying to rein in his temper.

"There's nothing to be gained by the two of you staying here longer," Joe said from behind him, approaching so quietly Evan hadn't heard the large man heading his way. "Tell Adrian to take you home. Jenna and I will finish up."

Evan bristled at being ordered around, although his intuition sided with Joe. "All right. I hope it was worth the time away from my research."

When he returned to the gallery, Adrian was looking for him and visibly relaxed when Evan came into view.

"I was about to make good on my threat," Adrian said under his breath. "I think it's time to go. We've made our point—and we're attracting too much attention. And by 'we,' I mean 'you.'"

Evan didn't object as Adrian guided him toward the door, although he winced when Adrian touched the small of his back. He understood the performative importance of demonstrating that he was under Adrian's protection, but the gesture felt too intimate, too *claiming*.

He had a partner to rescue, a man he loved with his whole heart. So even the appearance of stepping out with Adrian as more than friends bothered Evan deeply.

"Relax. I just want to make sure no one decides to eat you for a midnight snack," Adrian said, leaning down to murmur in Evan's ear. "Just go along with me until we get to the car."

The valet brought the Maserati, and Adrian held the door for Evan. Once they were both inside, Evan tried to relax.

"What did you make of it?" Adrian asked as they drove away.

"Osborn stopped me on the way back from the restroom. Everything he said had plausible deniability, but he warned me off Cleveland with a veiled threat and suggested I should leave."

"Typical," Adrian said, rolling his eyes. "Just another entrepreneur who believes his own PR."

"What he said makes me sure Seth is still alive—for now. Did you get what you wanted out of dragging me there?" Evan asked.

Adrian nodded as he maneuvered through traffic. "Yes. Osborn clearly knew who you were. He went even further when he spoke to you at the end. It's not something we can take to court, but that doesn't take away the value. It confirms that Osborn's the one who kidnapped Seth, which should narrow the search."

Evan let his head fall back and closed his eyes. "That bit about me being eaten—you were kidding, right?"

"Mostly. We have agreements in place that are supposed to govern how vampires, werewolves, and the like behave toward humans. Most of the time, they're followed. But there are always those who believe that rules are for other people, and many of them were present tonight."

"Great."

"I can't take them all head-on," Adrian said. "Even Joe and Jenna can't. But trust the process, Evan. Joe and Jenna are building a case. I'm here to help. We'll find Seth."

"I hope so." *Because I will burn down every hell gate and Osborn along with them if something happens to him.*

7

SETH

"For someone on vacation, you stay up late and get up early," Jesse observed, bringing two cups of coffee with him as he sat across from Seth in the campground's snack bar/gathering center.

"I couldn't sleep," Seth replied. It wasn't a lie. His dreams had either been dark with portents of death or achingly erotic, with the dark-haired stranger fulfilling his fantasies. He figured he could deal with being groggy more than he could handle panic or blue balls.

Jesse pushed one of the cups toward him, no doubt noticing the three empty paper cups and a plate with a half-eaten breakfast burrito that littered the space next to Seth. "Find anything interesting while you're surfing the Net?"

"Lots of stuff—just not sure what to do with it."

Jesse leaned in. The community room dining hall was mostly empty except for a table of retirees playing cards at the far end. "Talk to me, Seth. I don't know whether you've got PTSD, or if you're just bored with the family vacation—"

"I'm not bored," Seth replied and meant it. His time in the military had taught him how fragile life was, and he treasured every moment with his family. "But something weird is going on, and I don't think it's from what I saw overseas."

"Tell me."

"You'll think I'm nuts."

Jesse grinned, that annoying little brother smile that Seth secretly loved. "I'll think you're nuts anyhow. What have you got to lose?"

Seth sighed and then decided to be honest. "You know how déjà vu is a feeling that you've done something before when you haven't? I feel like I've got two lives—the one I'm living here with you and Mom and Dad, plus another somewhere else, where things are different. And sometimes, the two lives intersect. That's when I see something that looks completely real—and then it vanishes."

"Like the gun you saw that wasn't there."

"It was solid and real before it vanished," Seth said.

"But no one else saw it." Jesse's voice was neutral, not accusing. Seth still felt it like a jab to the heart.

"I saw what I saw. There've been other things I didn't mention. I look around the RV, and I see sigils—magical symbols—marked everywhere, but I know you can't see them. Sort of like they're in black light paint, and only I have the way to make them glow," Seth confided.

"And sometimes, I know things. A strange word, an incantation, a bit of lore will pop into my mind, and I know it's true; I know it belonged to another me. But I'm not *him*," he continued.

Jesse regarded Seth thoughtfully. "Maybe that's for the best. Maybe things didn't turn out well for the other-you. This could be your do-over. Or...your heaven."

Seth thought about that and shook his head slowly. "A man keeps showing up. I don't recognize him, but I know I should. He's important."

"Important, how? Friend? Enemy? Lover?"

"I think...I care for him. A lot."

"Well, that explains why you didn't go for the guy I fixed you up with."

Seth nodded. "Yeah. It just felt wrong."

"Gotta respect you for not cheating on someone you don't remember."

Seth made a face. "Thanks...I think."

"Seriously—what do you want to do? Mom and Dad think you need to go see a therapist."

"It probably wouldn't hurt—but I might fry the poor guy's circuits."

"Yeah, if you go talking about intersecting timelines, it's not going to go well," Jesse said. "How are you going to figure this out?"

"I think I need to see a psychic," Seth said. "Someone legit. Maybe they'll pick up something from my aura and know what to do."

"What about your phantom boyfriend?" Jesse asked.

"I'll figure it out. I don't know what we are to each other here or if he's actually real."

Jesse sobered. "Are you going away? Does solving your mystery mean you vanish into thin air?"

Seth wanted to reassure him, tell him that he wouldn't disappear, wouldn't leave his family. "I want to say that I won't, but I don't know."

Jesse nodded, and while he looked sad, he didn't seem surprised. "We need to make sure you're where you belong. Let's find a psychic who's the real thing."

Seth refused to lose time with his parents or Jesse. Knowing that their chance to be together was probably limited, he didn't want to miss a minute. For the rest of the day, he happily followed the itinerary his mother and Jesse had put together, playing tourist in downtown Richmond, walking along the river, and seeing the Iron Fronts—a row of historic buildings with elaborate facades made of metal.

They fed the squirrels in Capitol Park, went to the gardens at Maymont, and toured a mansion brought over brick-by-brick from England.

All the while, Seth couldn't shake the sense that he had done many of the same things before with someone else. An impending sense of danger dogged him, and he couldn't help continually glancing around, looking for threats.

His parents were too caught up in the history of the places they visited to notice, but Jesse never missed anything.

"What's up?" Jesse asked, bumping Seth on purpose.

Seth shook his head. "I've been here. It was important—essential. I saved someone, and it changed everything. Maybe—the dark-haired stranger." *Evan*.

Jesse clapped a hand on his shoulder. "Whatever you need to do, I'm with you."

Peace washed over Seth, the way Jesse's unconditional acceptance always made him feel. It smoothed off the rough edges of his anxiety and glossed over the doubts, fears, and recrimination. "Thanks." He tried to sound off-handed, afraid of how much it meant to him. He had a feeling that Jesse already knew.

"I want to see the pump house at James River Park," his mother said as they finished their tour at Maymont. "Before we do the museum and the botanical garden."

Jesse groaned. "Leave it to Mom to create the vacation forced march from hell. We will see every notable location in Richmond or die trying."

Seth laughed. "It's not that bad. We're together, having fun."

"I'm calling this the 'Vlad the Impaler Tour' on social media," Jesse said. "I need to start whistling that song from that old movie Dad made us watch—the one with the forced march where they blow up the bridge."

"Mom just likes to make the most of our time," Seth said, as Linda enthusiastically lectured Brian on some bit of trivia that had caught her fancy. Brian's look of fond forbearance struck a chord in Seth.

I want that. Someone who still thinks I'm fantastic even when I talk their ear off. Someone who will indulge my crazy vacation planning because it makes me happy. Someone who loves me the way Dad loves Mom.

They reached the pump house, and as soon as it came into view, Seth recoiled. "I don't think we should go any closer." He tried not to let his voice shake. He *remembered* being here, in a place he'd never seen before but knew intimately. He could see the large ruined ballroom on the second floor and the huge, disassembled mechanical apparatus for the river pump on the first floor.

Seth remembered the ghost too. How it had chased and nearly caught him.

"I don't think it's wise to go inside." God, how he hated making his warnings sound bland and unlikely to induce panic. All Seth wanted to do was scream, *"Go back! It's not too late. Stop now!"*

"It's supposed to be haunted," Jesse added, backing him up.

"I want to see the ballroom. They used the top floor for social events back in the day," Linda replied.

"It's locked except for occasional tours," Seth told them, unsure how he knew. "If they aren't running now, we're out of luck."

"Let's go to Hollywood Cemetery instead," Jesse suggested. "There's a mausoleum that's supposed to belong to the 'Richmond Vampire.' Plus, a lot of famous people are buried there."

Seth groaned inside, not wanting to go. But his instincts didn't warn him away from danger. Instead, he just felt an aversion, as if something important but unpleasant had happened there.

"Sounds like a plan," Linda said, while Brian let out an exaggerated moan, tempered by his smile.

Seth didn't hate going to the cemetery, but he was jumpy and hypervigilant. While his mother and father commented on the well-known names on the monuments, and Jesse snapped photos of the more unusual markers, Seth kept watch.

"You don't look like you're having fun," Linda observed, walking up to stand beside him. "You're standing like a bodyguard."

Seth forced a smile. "Old habits. I saw something online about purse snatching and pickpockets taking advantage of tourists. It *is* rather deserted here. I just didn't want you to be bothered."

Linda stretched up to kiss him on the cheek. "My soldier. You're on vacation too. It's okay to relax."

"I'm trying." Seth wasn't lying. He didn't know how to let go of the memories—or hallucinations—that were tied so strongly to the places they had visited. *It's almost like out of all the places we could go, something keeps drawing us to the ones from my visions.*

"I know it's hard to switch gears," she said, gently rubbing between his shoulder blades with her knuckles like she used to when he was little. He realized how much he had missed her touch while he was away.

"I know that you and Jesse are all grown up now, and you're building lives of your own," Linda said. "Maybe you'll join us now and then for vacation, but you'll get busy. I'm glad to have a family road trip—like it used to be—before that happens."

Seth felt overcome by emotion, far more than the situation warranted, and he had to swallow a few times to speak. "Me too, Mom. Thanks for this."

He noticed that while their dad was wandering among the monuments, focused on the epitaphs, Jesse hung back, doing something on his phone. Linda wandered away to join Brian, and Seth caught up to Jesse.

"What's up?"

"Just looking for that psychic you wanted," Jesse said. "We need to figure out what's going on so one way or the other, you can be fully present."

Jesse's effort on his behalf meant a lot to Seth. "Did you find someone?"

His brother nodded. "Maybe. Out of all the ones listed, I found a few who had comments that made me think they could have some ability—and not just be good at social engineering or reading behavior clues. I mean, if you have a person's name before the appointment, it doesn't take much to go find their social media accounts and read up on what's been going on in their lives."

"Makes sense."

"But the woman with the best comments knew things that the clients swore they never posted online—or even told anyone. Not the kind of stuff you could guess, either," Jesse replied. "I figured that while Mom and Dad go to the garden after breakfast tomorrow, we could go see 'Madam Annabelle.'"

Seth snorted. "Seriously? That's her name?"

"Probably not her real one, but I can't blame her for having a stage name. I imagine she runs into a lot of crazies in her business."

"I'll try not to be one of those people."

"You're not crazy, Seth," Jesse said in a warm tone. "Part of you knows things that haven't been revealed, and the rest of you needs to figure what's missing."

"When did you get so smart?" Seth asked as Jesse slipped his phone into his pocket.

"While you were gone. Although I learned everything that mattered from my big brother."

~

AFTER BREAKFAST THE NEXT MORNING, LINDA AND BRIAN HEADED OFF FOR the Ginter Botanical Garden while Jesse and Seth drove down to the Fan District to visit Madam Annabelle.

Seth felt nervous. Riding his Hayabusa helped. Jesse wasn't entirely comfortable on a motorcycle, which was the only thing that kept him from opening up the throttle and flying down the highway.

He stopped at the curb beside a modest, older home. A neatly lettered sign in the front yard proclaimed, *Psychic. Aura Readings, Tarot, Energy Work, Séances.*

"You think Madam Annabelle is the real thing?" Seth asked skeptically as they walked toward the house.

"Guess we'll see, huh?"

A grandmotherly woman with pale skin, light blue eyes, and a curly perm met them at the door. She wore a cardigan sweater over a T-shirt and jeans. Seth's notion that Annabelle would be swathed in bright silks and bohemian fashion made him reconsider his expectations.

"Thank you for being on time," Annabelle said. She looked from one brother to the other. "You did right bringing him here," she said, looking directly at Jesse.

Annabelle turned to Seth and blanched. "Oh, you sweet boy! Come on in. We need to talk."

As they followed her into the living room, Seth turned to Jesse. "What did you tell her?"

Jesse shook his head. "Nothing. I swear. I didn't want to bias anything. I just said that you were under a lot of stress, and I thought this would help."

The modern, comfortable living room didn't resemble the cloth-draped, garish "reading room" Seth expected. Annabelle motioned for Seth and Jesse to take a seat on the couch, and she sat in a wing chair.

"I don't know what—" Seth began.

"You don't belong here," Annabelle cut him off. "This isn't your time. I don't mean this appointment. I mean this..." She gestured to indicate everything around them. "This world. You're not from here, but something is keeping you here. Doesn't want to let you go. Now why would that be?"

Seth shook his head. "I don't know."

"What do you mean?" Jesse asked, looking like he'd gotten more than he bargained for.

Annabelle turned her attention to Jesse. "You want to believe him, but you're worried. Good on you for sticking with him. Your parents, they aren't so sure."

She looked at Seth. "You have an enemy. He has hidden the truth. You're happy here, but if you stay, you will die." Her eyes narrowed, "It will also cost the life of someone close to you." Annabelle's compassionate expression almost undid Seth. "I don't envy you."

Jesse looked stricken as if he had already lost Seth.

"What do I do?" Seth felt heartbroken. He had missed his family with a bone-deep longing, especially Jesse. Being home with them was a dream come true. But Seth couldn't ignore the growing sense that the handsome stranger was essential and the key to discovering the truth.

"I can't tell you that," Annabelle said. "You will need to decide for yourself."

Seth thanked the psychic and paid her. As he and Jesse walked to the door, she laid a hand on his arm.

"You will know what is real and what is not when you look for the holes," she told him. "The gaps will guide you to your true home."

"Thank you." Seth felt a shiver run down his spine. He managed a polite smile, although Jesse looked wrecked.

They walked outside into the cold. "Talk to me, bro," Seth begged.

"I don't understand," Jesse said, clearly upset. "I thought she might tell you that there was something that happened to you when you were overseas, maybe a trauma you were blocking and didn't realize it. But this...how can you be torn between two realities?"

Seth shook his head. "I don't know. It sounds like something out of a movie. Did I disappear from the other life? Are they running in parallel?"

"Or are you in a coma, and one of the lives is a dream?"

Jesse's comment shook Seth. *Is there truth in what he just said? Is that why my hand is shaking? Do I know something on some subconscious level and don't realize it?*

"Then it must be the other life I've dreamed because this is real. Solid." He reached out and squeezed Jesse's shoulder.

Jesse looked unpersuaded. "What if it's not? What if you belong to the other life? I saw a movie about someone whose fate split off in two directions because of a car accident. In one version, he died, and in the other, he didn't."

Seth slung an arm around Jesse's shoulders. He could see how rattled his brother was by the visit to the psychic. "We'll figure things out."

"Seth, you don't understand. I spent the whole time you were in the Army scared shitless that you wouldn't make it back," Jesse confessed. "I prayed every night and lit candles—and I'm not religious. I followed the news, wondering which battles you were in and whether you'd come home alive."

Seth felt a pang of guilt. He realized how impulsive he had been when he enlisted and how little thought he had given to the impact on his family. If there was any single thing in his life he would do differently, he wouldn't have run away from a broken heart.

"I'm so sorry."

"I don't want to lose you again. But your two lives are bleeding together. That means only one of them is going to last. And forgive me, but I want it to be this one—the one where we're together, and you're home and safe," Jesse confessed.

"I want that too," Seth assured him. But his mind went to the dark-haired stranger, and he wondered if he had to choose, what his heart would decide.

8

EVAN

"YOU DIDN'T HAVE TO COME."

"I wasn't going to let you do this on your own," Parker maintained stubbornly.

"I don't want you to get hurt," Evan replied without looking at his brother. They were just about to slip through a cut in the chain-link fence around the abandoned observatory, and he felt guilty for letting his younger brother tag along.

"And I don't want you to get killed." Parker raised his chin defiantly.

Evan knew that trying to force his brother to stay at the RV would just result in more danger, since Parker would follow him anyway.

"I want my partner back." Evan saw the stress of the past few days in his face every time he looked in the mirror. His decision not to shave was partly to save time and also because he didn't like looking at the haunted-eyed stranger in his reflection.

He and Seth were coming up on their one-year anniversary—a year that had taken Evan's world and shaken it like a snow globe. He'd accepted that the supernatural was real—and learned to do some magic of his own. He'd fought off creatures he used to think belonged only in horror movies and discovered a secret network of people with special abilities who risked everything to keep the world safe from threats most people couldn't imagine in their wildest nightmares.

Evan had also found out what it was like to fall head-over-heels in love, to be an outlaw, and to live on the run. He'd learned how to do emergency stitches and blood transfusions, exorcisms, and wardings.

Because of Seth.

After losing his home and family and then surviving an abusive ex-boyfriend, Evan had begun to doubt that he would ever find his "forever person." Then Seth had saved his life, swept him off his feet, and brought him into a life of secrets and danger.

Now, Evan had to balance saving the next sacrifice victim and rescuing his partner. Despite his training and on-the-job experience, Evan had to fight feeling that the quest was too much.

Seth is out there. And I'm going to find him and bring him home.

He dared not linger on the truth that the longer Seth remained missing, the less likely they would be to find him alive.

THIS TIME, EVAN PARKED SEVERAL BLOCKS AWAY FROM THE ABANDONED observatory. "Last chance to change your mind," he told Parker.

"Not happening," Parker replied, tipping his head as if he was daring Evan to lock him in the truck.

Evan swore under his breath. "Okay—but stay close, and if anything goes wrong—run."

He shouldered into a backpack that held everything he needed to work the spell for opening the anchor's hiding place. Evan also had salt, holy water, and a shotgun with rock salt rounds. He hoped none of those would be needed, but he wasn't taking any chances.

The chain-link fence had been cut in so many places it was unlikely anyone would bother to patch them. Evan selected the best hidden spot and led the way. He would have preferred to wait for darkness, but they didn't have the luxury of time.

They kept low, glancing around to make sure no one was watching. Evan used his unlock spell to open the back door and passed a flashlight to Parker, grabbing one for himself as well.

"Take this," he said, handing the shotgun to Parker. "It's filled with rock salt rounds. I know that you can handle it after all the times Grandad took us shooting."

"Who am I supposed to shoot?"

"Ghosts, if they bother us. People, if they try to stop me. As long as you're not firing point blank, that should hurt like hell but not kill someone. Once I start the spell to open the medallion, I can't stop. I'll be vulnerable. You need to protect me."

Parker met his gaze. "You trust me."

Evan nodded. "I'm trusting you with my life—and Seth's."

"I won't let you down."

"I know you won't."

When they reached the medallion in the floor, Evan wasted no time setting out the ritual elements. He had repeated the steps in his mind until he had them memorized. The spell itself was fairly simple, but obscure. Teag and Travis had assured him that his minor ability was more than sufficient.

Evan hoped with all his heart that they were right.

Parker turned his back on Evan to watch the doorway, looking over his shoulder with an expression that mingled fascination and fear.

I know that this is minor magic. A real witch can do so much more. But in Parker's eyes, this is damning. I know what we were taught about witches and anything supernatural. He may change his mind about me once he's seen what I can do.

Evan couldn't dwell on that now. He couldn't be sure that they would remain uninterrupted, and he doubted that if they were caught, he would get another chance in time to save Seth.

He set down a warded circle and lit candles at the four quarters. In the center, over the medallion, Evan combined plant powders and dried leaves in a silver bowl to amplify the spell. He spoke the incantation and tossed a match into the mixture.

A streak of green flame shot upward. Beneath the bowl, the medallion rotated. Evan waited until its motion stopped before releasing the magic and reaching forward to lift the sigil-marked disk from its place.

He shined his flashlight into the compartment and withdrew a cloth-wrapped bundle, which he shoved into his backpack to examine later. Evan debated for a few seconds and then replaced the medallion, hiding the theft. Then he gathered the ritual materials and stood.

"Let's get out of here," he said to Parker, who was watching the door with the shotgun trained on the entrance.

They hurried back the way they came, checking at every turn to see if they had been followed. Just before they reached the end of the last corridor before the entrance, Evan held up a hand for Parker to stop. Whether it was instinct or magic, Evan felt certain they were walking into a trap.

"Take this," Evan said, shrugging out of the backpack and handing it to Parker. He pulled out his truck and RV keys, as well as his phone, and shoved them into Parker's hands.

"Go to the RV and stay there. My phone has the same code as always. Call Joe Mack, and tell him there's trouble. He's in my contacts," Evan whispered. "He'll know what to do."

Parker looked like he was going to argue when a noise from near the exit put them both on high alert. He gave a curt nod, then went back the way they had come, extinguishing his flashlight and slinking in the shadows.

"I know you're in there," Officer Nelson called out. "I got a tip someone broke in, and you're my top suspect. Come out, and we can do this easy."

Once Evan knew Parker was out of sight, he figured keeping Nelson busy would buy his brother time to get away.

"I'm coming out. Don't shoot," Evan called, hoping that Nelson hadn't been completely controlled by Osborn and didn't intend to concoct a story to justify shooting him dead.

"Keep your hands where I can see them," Nelson warned.

Evan moved slowly, hands in the air. Nelson stood between him and the entrance, gun drawn.

"You're under arrest. We're going down to the station."

"On what charges?" Evan hoped he could buy Parker time.

"Breaking and entering, trespassing—that's for starters," Nelson replied and started into the Miranda warning.

Evan let Nelson cuff him, knowing he could unlock the handcuffs with a word. He didn't resist and felt relieved that Nelson appeared to be alone.

Nelson manhandled him toward the squad car. "Where's your truck?"

"Took a ride-share," Evan lied. "Parking's a bitch around here."

"I don't know why you picked Cleveland to cause trouble, but it stops right now," Nelson muttered.

"Patrolling the observatory is the most important public safety issue in the city?" Evan asked with faux innocence.

"Broken windows lead to bigger things," the cop replied.

Evan tried not to fidget. He'd never been arrested before, and while he had faith in his friends to free him, he didn't know how far under Osborn's sway Nelson was. *Plenty of witnesses have had tragic "accidents" in police custody. Let's hope I'm not one of them.*

He and Seth had taken pains to clean up after themselves in the fights against the other witch disciples. They and their friends monitored APBs and BOLOs to make sure they weren't going to show up on post office bulletin board "wanted" posters. Still, Evan worried that they might have overlooked something or been caught on video in a way that linked them to those events.

Guess I'll find out.

Evan had watched enough police dramas to expect a second round of Miranda, and to be fingerprinted, booked, and charged with a crime. Instead, Nelson put him in an interrogation room and handcuffed him to the table.

"I want to know why you're showing up like a bad penny," the cop demanded, looming over Evan.

"I want my lawyer," Evan replied, doing his best to keep his voice calm.

"Just answer my questions, and you're free to go," Nelson said.

Evan knew better. "I want my lawyer," he repeated.

Nelson slammed his fist on the table. Evan doubted there was anyone watching behind the mirrored glass, or if there was, maybe they were also under the witch disciple's sway. He noticed Nelson did not have a body cam to record this. "Caught you trespassing twice, plus breaking and entering. And you were at the library when something happened to the librarian. Maybe you attacked her?"

"Lawyer."

"You don't get it," Nelson hissed. "You're tinkering with something that's a lot bigger and badder than you are, and you're going to bring holy hell down on all of us if you don't back the fuck off."

Interesting. Does he know or suspect something about Osborn? Is this his ham-fisted way to keep the situation from escalating?

The door opened, and a woman in a dark, all-business pantsuit walked in. Evan recognized Jenna Anderson, and sat back to watch the fireworks.

"Who are you?" Nelson demanded.

Jenna flashed her badge. "Secret Service. I'm here to take Mr. Malone off your hands."

Nelson smirked at Evan. "What's he wanted for?"

"He's not 'wanted.' He's in protective custody. Return his belongings. I've already spoken to your superiors." She glanced at Evan, just long enough to assure that there were no visible injuries. "Let's go."

Evan did his best to keep a neutral expression and remained silent as Nelson removed the handcuffs. He looked like he might pop a gasket, but Evan swore he saw fear and not malice in the cop's eyes. *He knows something. But is he working for Osborn or trying to work around him?*

Since he had given everything except spare change to Parker back at the observatory, checking him out went quickly. Neither he nor Jenna spoke until they got into a black sedan driven by Joe Mack.

"Thank you for coming for me," Evan said, finally feeling the shakes hit now that he was safe.

"Are you okay?" Jenna asked.

Evan swallowed hard and nodded. "Yeah. Nelson had a lot of bluster, but he didn't try to hurt me. He's a descendant—Osborn's next victim. And I don't know if he's figured out what's going on, but I think he suspects something isn't right."

"Your brother kept a level head," Joe told him. "He's safe at the RV. Were you planning on telling us about him?"

"I didn't know he was going to show up," Evan replied. "Long story, dysfunctional family. He called and said he thought he was being watched. I told him to come because I needed to protect him."

"You didn't wonder if he'd been compromised?" Jenna asked in a sharp tone.

"I wondered—but I haven't seen any evidence to support that," Evan replied. "We were always close, even after I left. He insisted on coming with me today. Turned out to be a good thing."

WHEN EVAN RETURNED TO THE RV, PARKER GREETED HIM WITH A frightened hug. "Thank God. I was afraid they'd find a reason to keep you there—or hurt you."

Evan disengaged with a smile, surprised and grateful for Parker's concern. "You did good, calling Joe. One of his friends with clout sprung me, which should make Officer Nelson and his cronies think twice before they try something like that again."

That's when Evan noticed the array of components, wires, and tools spread out over the table. "What have you been up to? I've only been gone a few hours."

"I was thinking that there are times when it would be cool if you could relay a video feed back to someone at your home base," Parker replied.

"I have an action camera, but they're expensive, so I couldn't get many when I stopped on the way here. I rigged a doorbell video camera to a battery and then worked out how to bring up multiple feeds on one computer screen, like in the movies." Parker's pride was clear in his voice.

"Dude, that's genius," Evan said, truly impressed, though he was bothered that his brother made a stop at a hardware store instead of going straight to the camper.

Parker shrugged, looking embarrassed.

"I knew that engineering class would come in handy," Evan added. He could tell that Parker was pleased by his admiration.

"This is perfect," Evan went on. "Sometimes we have the ear links and a shared comm system if we're sneaking into the bad guy's lair.

But that stuff was always borrowed. What you've built is something we can use again and again. This is awesome."

Parker's cheeks reddened at the praise. "It wasn't hard."

"It would have been for me."

"Yeah, well. I can't shoot fire, so I need to be useful somehow since I'm eating your food and taking up space here," Parker replied.

Evan shook his head. "You don't have to earn your keep, although I'm grateful for what you've built. You're my brother. You always have a place here."

Parker looked down. "I had no idea what you were dealing with, I swear. You've got to believe me—I would have come sooner if I'd known."

Evan walked to the fridge, retrieving two beers. He set one in front of Parker and plunked himself down on the leather couch on the other side of the RV, facing his brother. Then Evan reached for the remote and turned on the electric fireplace.

"Fuck, after the day I've had, I just want to get buzzed and stare into the fire." Evan sighed. "I didn't want you to know about the magic and the murders. If I'd had my way, Seth and I would have gotten rid of all the witch disciples, and none of the other descendants would have ever had to find out."

"Now that I do, I can't just pretend it's not real," Parker said. "I want to help."

"Absolutely not," Evan snapped.

Parker raised his hands in a gesture of truce. "Hear me out. You said you've got hacker allies and witches and whatnot. But you don't have a tech person or you'd have already been geared up with cameras and headsets and all that. I can be your gadget guy. I'll be out of the line of fire—in fact, I can be anywhere. Monitoring your feed when you go into a dicey situation. Making sure you have the equipment you need."

Parker's chin set in the expression Evan remembered from his "difficult" early teenage years. "The people who were murdered were my relatives too. This is my fight as much as yours."

"You've got to finish college. You have a job," Evan argued.

"*Jobs*—plural—and none of them pays more than minimum wage.

I'm doing mostly online classes, and I can do that anywhere. Besides, you said I wasn't safe in Columbus."

Damn, I hate it when he's right. Evan paused and then nodded. "Alright, you're in. But you stay out of the line of fire, got that?"

Parker gave him a snarky salute. "I'll be right here in front of the computer, just like in all the heist movies. Do I need a code name?"

"Would it make you happy?" *Actually, that's not a bad idea—keeps Parker more anonymous in case anyone hacks the audio.*

"Yes, actually. How about just 'Gadget' for short? That way, when you need something, you can say—"

"Go, go, Gadget!" both brothers said in unison, laughing at the reference to a favorite childhood movie despite their dire situation.

Parker grinned, making it clear that jerking Evan's chain was at least part of the appeal.

I forgot how much I missed having Parker around. It's going to make it that much worse when Seth and I have to leave.

"How can this work when we don't know where Seth is?" Evan asked Johnny Laveccia as they sat around a small table in a back room at the Hathaway Theater speakeasy. Joe Mack leaned against the door, making sure they weren't disturbed. Parker sat in a chair by the wall, eyes wide.

Johnny had his best manager covering for him. Evan could barely hear the rumble of voices beyond the thick door. He wondered if this room had served as a private gambling suite during Prohibition.

A thick pillar candle sat in the center of the table, which had been chalked with sigils and runes. Incense burned in a brazier, making Evan lightheaded.

An antique silver chalice held the potion Johnny assured Evan would enable him to find Seth and communicate with him regardless of distance. Evan didn't know what kind of magic the tracking spell used, but it required stronger power than he possessed, and he was grateful for Johnny's help.

He'd provided a few hairs from Seth's brush. Evan didn't care how the spell worked—as long as it assured him Seth was still alive and provided clues to help find him.

"Are you ready?" Johnny asked.

Evan nodded, even though his heart pounded in his throat and his palms sweated. "More than ready."

He'd seen séances in movies and wondered if this would be similar —only seeking a living person, not a ghost. *Please, let Seth be alive. I need to bring him back.*

Johnny lifted the chalice and drank. Evan accepted the cup from him, holding it with both hands.

"Drink the rest. We'll be connected as soon as it hits your system," Johnny told him.

Evan gulped it down, finding the mixture thick and bitter.

Johnny placed his hands flat on the table, fingers splayed. Evan did the same, positioning his so that the tips of their fingers touched. He felt a frisson like an electric spark at the contact.

"Whatever happens, don't break contact with me," Johnny warned. "I hope Seth is okay, but we don't know what you'll see. Whoever took him didn't have his best interests at heart."

Evan nodded. "I realize that. But I have to know. I'm going to bring him back, no matter what it takes."

Something glinted in Johnny's eyes, and Evan wondered if the witch had lost people of his own.

"My magic will connect you to his energy. I don't know how long we can hold the connection," Johnny warned.

Evan nodded, resolved to see this through. He closed his eyes and tried to relax, letting the strange sensations fill him that were awakened by the potion. He pictured Seth in his mind and made the image as real as possible, remembering every detail of his lover.

If I want to find him, maybe I should think of when we were truly joined together. Memories of making love flooded through him, leaving Evan sad and achingly hard. Seth was a thoughtful and generous lover, so different from the boyfriends Evan had before.

Evan focused on the details, remembering the most recent sex, then flashing back to their first night together, and from there, memories of so many special times.

"Open your eyes," Johnny told him. "Tell me what you see."

"I'm getting images; they jump from place to place," Evan reported. "A diner. Walking down the sidewalk. Except, wait—he's with someone. A man I don't recognize."

For a moment, Evan's heart thudded. *Was this a memory of an old lover? Someone who made Seth wish, deep inside, that they could have another chance?*

Then Evan noted the similarities between the two men and gasped when he connected the stranger's face with a photo in the trailer. "He's with his brother, Jesse. His *dead* brother."

"What?" Johnny sounded startled.

"Seth is home with his family. They all died because of one of the disciples, and he misses them terribly. He was very close to Jesse." Evan swallowed hard. "If they're all dead, do you think—"

"My magic is strong, but not powerful enough to see into the afterlife," Johnny assured him. "What you're probably seeing is an illusion where Seth is trapped—in his mind. What else do you see?"

"Time moves quickly in these images. He might think he's been there for weeks instead of days." Evan paused. "Can he see me?"

"Why do you ask?"

"Sometimes I think he spots me in the crowd. I can feel him watching me. Maybe it's my imagination—"

"It's possible," Johnny said, "but that would require an exceptionally strong bond between the two of you. That's our opening. If he can see you, maybe you can get him to understand that he's in a dream. If we can break the illusion, we might break Osborn's hold on him. If he's sleeping, or unconscious, that might help him wake up."

"Okay," Evan replied. "Then I've got a mission. This is the third day since he disappeared. The full moon is tomorrow. We've got to stop Osborn before he does the ritual."

They remained linked to Seth's illusion as long as Johnny could hold the connection. When it finally faded, Evan drew a deep, shaking breath.

"I had to let go," Evan whispered. "But I told him the truth. I told him to run."

"That's all you can do," Johnny replied, with more compassion than Evan would have expected.

Evan feared that if he responded he might break, so he cleared his throat. "Where are we on the plan? Time's run out."

"Adrian gave Jenna's people the data mining results," Joe reported. "And hacked the black box on Osborn's car. Your hunch appears to be right about the old rehab hospital. There's no reason for Osborn—or anyone else—to come and go, but he's visited twice in three days. Once Adrian figured that out, his people put a drone camera watching the doors. There are guards discreetly patrolling the outside, and a sketchy doctor who lost his license stops in every day."

"Like that's not ominous," Evan muttered.

"Jenna's got a Supernatural Secret Service team ready to go," Joe replied. "They'll go in and sweep the rehab hospital. If they find the missing people, they'll make sure they get care. You and Johnny and I will go into the old subway station and stop Osborn."

"We have the anchor. If we destroy it before we go, he'll be at a disadvantage." Evan pointed out.

"I've never chosen to go up against Osborn because I didn't have to," Johnny said. "If we can stop him from gaining the extra power from the ritual, we should be fairly well-matched. I'm confident enough to face off with him."

Joe and Evan exchanged glances, and Evan thought that Joe also harbored some doubts. *Who am I kidding? The plan sucks. But it's all we've got.*

"We've still got to get his amulet," Evan said. "Usually, the witch disciple keeps it on his person. It's a necklace or a watch fob or something he never goes without. He needs both to work the spell that summons his old master, Gremory."

"We'll figure it out," Joe told him.

Evan sighed. "You know that this could go wrong six ways to Sunday. It's insane."

"That's what I like about it," Joe replied. "When you're crazy, it's harder for people to predict what you're going to do. March into hell for a good cause and all that."

Evan was glad Joe walked out to the truck with him since Nelson was loitering nearby.

"Don't you have anything better to do?" Joe asked as the cop approached them.

Nelson shrugged. "Got an out-of-town troublemaker frequenting a bar with known Mob ties. Seems worth keeping tabs on."

"We're trying to save your life," Evan blurted, too angry and worried to filter his comments.

Nelson's eyes narrowed. "What did you just say?"

"Didn't you ever wonder why the oldest male of each generation dies young? Why the deaths are spread out by about twelve years? Didn't that ever strike you as odd?" Evan was on a roll, frustrated with Nelson's obstruction and his attitude.

"How do you—"

"Trace it back," Evan challenged. "The oldest of each generation died or disappeared all the way back to 1900–when your ancestor was a deputy to a sheriff in Brazil, Indiana, who hanged a warlock named Rhyfel Gremory."

"You're crazy," Nelson sputtered. "I ought to run you in for making veiled threats."

Joe took a step forward. "You'll do no such thing. He's not threatening you—he's trying to warn you that you're in danger."

"From what—a century-old serial killer?" The cop mocked, but Evan thought he saw a glint of fear in Nelson's eyes.

Evan started to reply, but Joe laid a hand on his shoulder. "Let it go," he advised. "He's not going to listen."

"Just—be careful," Evan said, hoping that Nelson at least thought he was sincere in his madness. "Even if you don't believe me, be extra cautious."

"Yeah, yeah. I'm always careful," Nelson muttered. "Now get going before I find a reason to haul you downtown."

Nelson walked off. Joe and Evan stood by the truck until the cop drove away.

"You tried," Joe said. "I'm not sure either of us thought Nelson would listen, but at least you gave it a shot."

Evan shook his head and sighed. "I think he's aware of the pattern, but it doesn't fit his cop training, and he doesn't know what to make of it. Maybe we can shut Osborn down before Nelson ever has to find out he's wrong."

Joe promised to be in touch as soon as he or his friends had news. Evan drove back to the campground with his head still spinning from the séance with Johnny. He was so deep in thought that he jumped when Travis Dominick's ring tone sounded on his phone through the truck's sound system.

"Hey, Travis. What do you have for me?"

"You wanted to know what happened to the witch disciple in St. Louis. Not sure how much it'll help, but from what we could find, Ronald Osborn was Willis's younger brother, from a family with a lot of witchy history," Travis told him.

"Osborn killed his own brother?" Evan knew he probably shouldn't have been surprised.

"More accurate to say that Willis got Ronald killed," Travis said. "Apparently, the brothers worked together on the supernatural drug trafficking business. Ronald was Willis's channel to the lower Midwest. They worked with the shadier shifter packs and vampire nests for distribution, and somewhere along the line, one of the packs decided to skim the profits. The Osborns confronted them, and when the fight was over, the pack was wiped out, and Ronald was dead."

"How long ago did that happen? And who replaced Ronald in the organization?" Evan asked, keeping his eyes on the road.

"Ronald died six months ago—right before the disappearances started," Travis replied. "And as far as anyone can tell, no one replaced him. Willis seems to be running everything through his distributors from Cleveland. Ronald's operation in St. Louis is completely gone."

"You brought up the disappearances." Evan frowned as he concentrated. "How is that related?"

"Just a theory, but it's possible Ronald was helping to sustain Willis. Without him, Willis had to leech energy from somewhere, and the lesser descendants were the next best option."

"That makes sense," Evan agreed. "I just wish it meant Willis was going to be easier to stop."

"I'll let you know what else we turn up," Travis promised. "And if you need us, Brent and I can be there in about two hours."

"Thank you," Evan told him, sure Travis could hear his worry and weariness. "Joe thinks he's got us covered, but I'll let you know if we need backup."

He ended the call after promising to keep Travis in the loop. When he pulled in beside the RV, Evan took a few minutes to compose himself before he was ready to answer Parker's questions.

Where are you, Seth? Hang in there. We're coming to get you.

9

SETH

"THERE SHOULD BE A THIN, FLEXIBLE PLASTIC TUBE FILLED WITH SALT THAT runs around every door, window, and vent," Seth said. "Protective symbols in UV paint on the undersides of the storage bin doors and inside the door panels to the truck and RV as well as the bike's saddlebags. Hidden compartments with weapons in several places. And lube in the cabinet and nightstand."

Jesse snickered at the last comment but sobered quickly. "What kind of person are you in that other place? Some kind of Zombie hunter? A ghostbuster like those guys on TV with the cool car?"

"Witch hunter," Seth answered before he had time to think about it. He felt as surprised as Jesse at the answer. "Not Zombies. Witches."

Jesse just stared at him. "Why? Wiccans don't hurt anyone."

Seth shook his head. "Not Wiccans. Real warlocks. Voldemort types."

"Dude, magic isn't real."

"Yet you suggested a psychic." Seth ran a hand through his hair. "I know that magic isn't real...but I also get these glimpses in my dreams where all kinds of things are real that shouldn't be."

That wasn't all that he saw in his dreams. Seth caught images of fights that ended bloody, explosions, and fire. Not to mention very detailed memories of making love to the dark-haired man. *He's not a stranger in that life. My lover. Partner.* The intense flash of emotions told Seth that their relationship was far more serious than a casual fling. *Fiancé? Husband?*

Then there was the memory of a doctor and a rundown hospital room with tubes, monitors, and restraints. *Did I get sent to a mental ward? Was I crazy in the other place? Is the insanity bleeding through?*

Jesse's gaze turned worried. "Maybe you should see a counselor."

Seth barked a rueful laugh. "So they can lock me up?" A shiver went down his spine and panic twisted his guts. *Guess I tried that, and it didn't go well in the other life.*

Tonight, Seth and Jesse sat on the roof of the RV with a pizza and a bucket of longnecks. Their parents had gone on a candlelight tour of one of the local historic mansions. The campground was fairly quiet, and the night was mild.

"I'll back you up, no matter what," Jesse said. "But I gotta tell you —this is starting to freak me out."

"You and me, both."

They sat in comfortable silence for a while, drinking beer and looking at the night sky, close enough their shoulders bumped. Seth felt a deep peace settle over him, soothing a bone-deep sadness.

"You're not going to stay," Jesse said quietly.

"I don't think I belong here," Seth answered, feeling like no matter what he chose, his heart would break.

"We're your family. You'll always belong here."

And Evan is my heart. "If this whole thing is just the fallout from an old head injury, nothing will change," Seth replied. "I'll feel like a total dumbass, and you'll have blackmail material for the rest of our lives."

"That man...he's important to you in the other place?"

Seth nodded. "He's my everything." He didn't have to think twice.

"Then we need to get you back to your man," Jesse said. "But I'm gonna miss you."

"Gonna miss you too."

"I always thought from the TV shows that when there were multiple timelines, there was more than one of you, living all the different variations of your life." Jesse kept staring at the sky, not turning to look at Seth. "Then you could have him, and we could have you."

"I wish."

"Are you going to tell Mom and Dad?"

Seth gave him the side-eye. "You're kidding, right? There's no way."

"You're just going to disappear?"

Seth looked down and picked at a loose thread on his jeans. "Not exactly. I thought I'd try to find Evan and the 'holes' the psychic mentioned. I keep dreaming about a corridor—maybe that's what she meant. But not until the last day of vacation—after I make it the best day ever. Something to remember."

Jesse gave a sharp nod, and Seth realized that his brother was trying not to cry. "It won't be the same without you."

"I'm sorry." Seth was quiet for a moment. "Just promise me something. Don't go to that 'hell gate' tunnel. Ever."

Jesse turned to him with a strange expression. "We went—in the other life. Something bad happened, didn't it?"

"Real bad,"

"Did I die?"

Seth felt like he wanted to throw up, and he wrapped his arms around his middle as the truth of Jesse's guess hit him. "Fuck."

Jesse paled. "That's why you hunt witches. For revenge."

As soon as the words were spoken, Seth knew the truth of them. "Jesse—"

"Maybe you're right where you're supposed to be. Maybe we're the ones who aren't supposed to be here," Jesse said before he finished off his beer.

Seth pulled out his phone on impulse, opening the search. *Jackson Evan Malone*, his mind supplied. He typed it in and held his breath.

"Oh, God," he whispered and held the screen so Jesse could see the obituary listing. The man in the photograph was the one in his dreams and the elusive stranger he glimpsed in the crowd.

Jesse took his phone and silently read down through the information. "He went missing on a hike, and his body was found near a trail."

"In this life, you didn't die, but Evan did."

"And in the other one, Evan lives, and I don't," Jesse concluded. "How do you keep seeing him here if he's dead?"

"Maybe somehow, my Evan is looking for me since magic is real on the other side." Seth's head spun, and his heart ached. *Lose my brother, keep my partner. Bury my lover, stay with Jesse. How can I choose?*

But as soon as the words crossed his mind, Seth knew the decision had already been made and that it was never really a choice at all.

"We've still got a few days left," Jesse said, popping the cap from another beer and handing it to Seth before taking one for himself. "Let's make the most of it. No regrets."

Seth threw himself into enjoying every moment of the remaining days of vacation. He and Jesse spent a day at Virginia Beach, chasing each other in the sand and gorging on seafood, and the next day, Linda led them on a foray to Monticello and Charlottesville. Each night, the four of them stayed up late watching movies and playing cards.

When he slept, Seth dreamed of fire, blood, and Evan.

After everyone else went to bed, Seth researched, trying to piece together the half-remembered clues his damaged memories provided. By the time the sun rose on the last day, Seth knew where he needed to go to get home.

That day, the family went to Colonial Williamsburg at Linda's urging, and it was bittersweet for Seth to see how much his Mom and Dad loved touring the historic area. He resolutely avoided thinking about what lay ahead.

Seth laughed and joked with Jesse and took a selfie of them wearing tri-cornered hats. They bought cookies and hot chocolate at the bakery, enjoyed going through the restored old houses, and ate in an old-time pub.

Throughout the day, Seth took every opportunity to hug his mother and find reasons to thank and compliment his father. He stuck close with Jesse, not wanting to miss a second of their time together.

On the ride back to the RV, everyone recounted their favorites from the day. Linda and Brian were tired but still bubbly over what they had seen. Seth did his best to keep up his part of the conversation. Jesse grew quiet, and Seth saw how sad his brother looked.

The Devil You Know

"Hey, it's not over yet," he murmured, giving Jesse's arm a nudge. Jesse chimed in on the discussion, but his smile looked forced.

Everyone tumbled out of the truck back at the campground, helping to carry packages filled with the things Linda and Brian bought in the stores and gift shops.

"That was a full day," Brian said as he put the bags on the kitchen table and stretched. "I'm heading for bed."

"Thanks for a great day," Seth said, stepping up and giving his dad a hug without providing a chance for the older man to avoid him.

Brian hugged back awkwardly. "Sure thing. Glad you had a good time."

Seth turned to his mom. "Okay if I kiss you goodnight? For all the times I wanted to and couldn't when I was in Afghanistan."

Linda returned his hug and stretched up to kiss him on the cheek. "We're just happy to have you home safe and sound," she told him. "Good night, you two."

Jesse waited until their parents headed to the master bedroom and closed the door. "What now?"

"I think I know where to find the 'hole' the psychic mentioned," Seth replied. "The Church Street Tunnel. I've had dreams about it. I think that I might have saved Evan's life there."

"Isn't it blocked off? You're just going to walk into a dark, abandoned railway tunnel at midnight and hope there aren't wild dogs or muggers—or worse—hanging out inside?" Jesse countered.

"If it's a passageway to another place, there won't be," Seth said, unsure why he was quite so certain.

"How do you plan to get there?"

"I've got the Hayabusa. It'll do."

"I'm coming with you," Jesse said as Seth gathered his things and shoved them into a backpack.

"No way."

"Take me with you, or I'll wake up Mom and Dad and tell them everything." Jesse stood in front of the door with his hands on his hips.

"Seriously?" Seth let out an exasperated sigh. He had forgotten how stubborn his brother could be when Jesse thought he had the high ground.

141

"Wanna try and see what happens?"

They glared at each other for a moment, and then Seth relented. "I don't want to fight with you."

"Then let me come. Besides, someone needs to bring the bike back if this harebrained scheme works," Jesse argued.

The idea of having even a little extra time with Jesse sealed the deal, although Seth feared for his brother's safety.

"Okay. But take this." He reached into his backpack and pulled out his service pistol and an extra clip. "Just in case we run into trouble."

"Aren't you going to need it if you actually do go through the looking glass?"

"Don't know. But if you're going with me, then you need to be able to protect yourself," Seth crossed his arms.

"Fine," Jesse returned.

"Fine," Seth echoed, just to be a pain in the ass.

Seth went to the kitchen and grabbed a pen and paper. *Mom and Dad—thanks for everything. I love you, Seth.* He left the note where his mom would be sure to see it.

"Going to write me a note too?" Jesse joked, but Seth could see the sadness in his eyes.

Seth pulled his brother into a bear hug. "No. I'm going to tell you flat out that I love you and that you're the best brother in the whole world and that I'm going to miss you like hell."

"Back atcha. Love you too, dweeb." Jesse's voice broke on the last word.

Seth thumped Jesse on the back one last time and reluctantly let go. "Come on before I lose my nerve."

"Would that be a bad thing?"

Half-remembered images flashed through Seth's mind. Most of them he couldn't quite place, but he knew they were important. "It might be," he replied. "I think we've saved people by stopping the witches."

"Then let's go do what you gotta do," Jesse told him, setting his jaw and blinking back tears.

Seth pushed the Hayabusa to the gates of the campground, so he didn't wake his parents with its rumble. He started the engine, Jesse climbed on behind him, and then they were flying through the night.

Even though it was late, Seth kept his speed down. He had no desire to get pulled over by a cop, especially with what was at stake. They wound through the darkened streets until they found the ravine that hid the old tunnel's east end. The glow of the streetlight didn't illuminate far beyond the damaged chain-link fence.

"You're nuts," Jesse said, staring into the darkness. "You're going to break a leg, and I'll have to haul your ass out of there."

Seth wondered what Jesse would remember once he was gone. *Or will the power that sent me here erase me completely from this version?*

"I've got my phone, so don't hang around up here by yourself," Seth warned.

"Screw that. I need to know if you get down to the bottom," Jesse replied.

Seth knew better than to argue and pulled his brother in for one last hug. Jesse hugged back hard enough Seth couldn't breathe—or maybe that was because he was trying not to cry.

"Just—be safe," Jesse told him when they finally stepped apart.

"You too. Remember what I said."

"No hell gate. Got it," Jesse replied with a watery smile.

Seth drew in a deep breath, shouldered his backpack, and slipped through a break in the fence. He was glad for his high-powered flashlight and solid boots. Before he got too far down the slope, Seth pulled his combat knife from his pack, keeping it in hand as he descended the steep, trash-filled slope.

All of his senses prickled on high alert. As his vision adjusted to the dark, Seth watched for movement or the glint of eyes. This wasn't hospitable territory for squatters, but he had no desire to run into feral dogs or rabid raccoons. In the distance, he heard the hum of traffic.

When Seth reached the bottom, he found a muddy trail leading to a rusted and bent chain-link fence.

The maw of the Church Hill Tunnel gaped wide and ominous, reminding Seth that a locomotive and its engine crew were forever entombed inside beneath a cave-in, beyond the concrete wall that—in his dreams—blocked off the passage.

Nothing about tonight felt normal.

The moon seemed too bright, and now that he had reached the entrance, the night had grown so silent around him that he swore all the sounds had been sucked out of the world.

But as Seth stared into the tunnel, he caught a glow where none should be, far down into its cavernous length. Gradually, the light intensified, and Seth saw the silhouette of a man striding toward him.

As the glow grew brighter, it revealed the man's face.

Evan.

"We don't have much time," Evan told him. "We've got to go. Take my hand, and no matter what you see or hear, don't let go. There are *things* inside that will try to stop us. Fight—but hang on."

Inside the tunnel, the light that illuminated the center of the passageway left shadowed areas along the stone walls. Their footsteps echoed.

The scratch of claws on rock sounded from the dark places, along with the wet slurp of something moving through the mud.

We're not alone. Did I really think it would be easy to leave?

"Keep moving," Evan told him. "We've got to get to the other side."

That confirmed Seth's suspicion that tonight magic made the tunnel into a portal.

Creatures slunk from the shadows to block their way—huge, misshapen black dogs with red eyes and long fangs. They were easily as large and solid as a full-grown man, covered with matted, dirty dark hair.

Grims a memory supplied, naming the beasts. At least a dozen of the monsters emerged, circling him and Evan like a wolf pack on the hunt.

Evan squeezed his hand, reminding Seth not to let go. "The warlock sent them to stop you from coming back," Evan said. "We've got to get past them to the door in the center of the bright light. If you die here, you die for real—so just don't."

Strong, sinewy bodies sprang at them, teeth bared. Full-throated growls echoed like the rumble of a freight train. The *grims* snapped and snarled, trying to knock Seth and Evan to the ground. Seth knew if they went down, those fangs would tear open their throats, and the long claws would rip them to pieces.

"Fight—but keep moving toward the far end," Evan ordered. Fighting one-handed was a challenge, but Seth hadn't come this far to fail. He jabbed and swung at the hounds with the wicked sharp blade, doing his best to keep them at bay.

One of the *grims* launched itself at Seth, more than a hundred pounds of muscular monster. Seth thrust his blade up, piercing its heart. Evan slashed with his machete, slitting the throat of the *grim* closest to him and spraying them both with hot blood.

All the while, the two men slowly shifted closer to the exit despite the *grims'* attempt to herd them back the way they came.

"They can fight all night—but we can't." Seth huffed. He was soaked with the *grim's* black blood but hadn't been bitten. Four of the *grims* were down, but eight remained.

"We'll make it," Evan assured him.

"We'd better," Seth replied, although he had doubts. They could die in this tunnel, trapped between realities. Knowing that Evan had come for him meant everything.

"The door won't stay open forever. We've got to get to it before the magic fades," Evan told him.

"Can we outrun them?" Seth asked, fearing he knew the answer.

Evan shook his head. "Only as a last resort—and the odds won't be in our favor."

Seth felt like a stag ringed by wolves. The pack moved in uncanny unison as if they shared a mind. Two of the beasts lunged. Seth dodged and dropped to his knees, then surged up with the knife and drove it through the creature's throat and into its skull. He kicked the body loose of his blade, never letting go of Evan's hand.

If they had all night and boundless energy, they might fight their way clear. But the glow at the far end of the tunnel had begun to dim. He didn't want to miss the chance to go home, and he sure as hell wasn't willing to let Evan get stranded here with him.

Gunshots echoed like thunder as Jesse emerged from the shadows. One after another, the *grims* fell.

The last two *grims* attacked in a flurry of fur, claws, and teeth. Seth and Evan were ready, beheading one and eviscerating the other. The beasts collapsed in bloody heaps.

"Go!" Jesse ordered. "I'll keep anything from stopping you. Run!" Jesse slammed a fresh clip into Seth's gun, then he grinned and saluted.

That was the image of Jesse that Seth took with him into the maelstrom of light and magic that burned like a furnace at the end of the passageway. Still gripping Evan's hand hard enough to bruise, Seth felt a chill of primal fear as he stared into the glowing portal.

"We run at it, like we expect it to yield, and it does," Evan told him. "Ready when you are."

Seth mustered his courage, grieving because he was leaving Jesse and ecstatic that Evan had not forgotten him.

"Let's do this," Seth said, meeting Evan's eyes. "To Infinity—" he yelled as they jumped hand in hand into the blinding brilliance.

"—and beyond!" Evan echoed.

Cold light overwhelmed Seth, and when he came to his senses, he woke in the rundown clinic from his nightmares, cuffed to the dented railing of a hospital bed.

"Evan?" he whispered tentatively in the gloom.

No answer came.

Beeping monitors replaced the snarl of *grims*, and their screens provided faint light in an otherwise darkened room. Seth pulled the IV needle out of his arm and winced as he removed a catheter, which made it clear that his kidnapper expected him to be left unattended for long periods.

Seth had no difficulty slipping his cuffs. He sat up and took in his surroundings.

Where the fuck am I? And where's Evan?

The building obviously hadn't been maintained in a long time. Paint peeled from the ceiling, and mold blossomed on crumbling plaster. The smell of dust and mildew filled the air.

Shit. I'm lucky I didn't wake up in a bathtub full of ice, missing a kidney. But this is a close second.

Seth could make out half a dozen occupied beds in the gloom, each surrounded by monitors and IV poles.

I bet I've found the missing descendants. He remembered the strange moments in his dreams when the odd "accountant" showed up, looking down on him with condescension.

Osborn. The man in my dreams matches his pictures. I remember getting walloped back at the library—and then I woke up with my folks, and Jesse was still alive. A wave of grief hit him, and he took a deep breath and pushed it back.

Fuck—did Osborn send us all to our happy places so we couldn't fight whatever he's doing to our bodies?

Seth's head swam. A glance confirmed that he wore the same clothes as when he got jumped, and he felt a surge of relief that he wasn't in a bare-assed hospital gown. He zipped up his fly. According to the date on the monitor screen, he'd been out for four days.

Shit. Evan's probably panicked. And tonight is the full moon. I've got to get these people out of here before Osborn works his ritual to power up.

He got rid of the monitors that were stuck to his skin and silenced the alarms, then walked on shaky legs toward the next bedridden victim.

Seth knew he had to hurry. *Monitors are...monitored. The countdown to getting caught started the moment I broke the feed.*

Seth recognized the man in the nearest bed as James Butler, who had vanished four months ago. He had been healthy and vibrant in the pictures circulated online, but the pallid, gaunt figure barely resembled his photographs. Desperate to assure that Evan was not one of the kidnap victims, Seth checked the other beds, but to his relief, his partner wasn't there.

Is Osborn a vampire? Seth didn't see puncture wounds or any evidence of bloodletting. *Some sort of psi-vamp, maybe? Or can he use his magic to siphon energy?*

He'd have to figure that out later.

Seth found his shoes tossed into a corner, another indicator to his mind that his captor never intended for him to leave alive. He vaguely remembered leaving his messenger bag in the reserved room at the library. He'd taken his phone, knife, and hex bags, only to be drugged by regular goons who removed his protections so a witch could whammy him. Seth swore under his breath at how easily he'd fallen for the trap.

A bin on a nearby table held cellphones and wallets from his fellow victims. Seth tried all the phones. Three were dead. He couldn't guess the password on two, but the third opened to "1-2-3-4" and still had enough battery for a 911 call—as soon as he had a signal.

Seth glanced around for a weapon and settled for a broken wooden chair leg. The locked corridor door yielded to his "unlock" spell, and its tumblers clicked open. He checked the hallway, relieved to find it empty.

He needed to save the others, but after four days of whatever Osborn had dosed him with, he was going to be lucky to get down the stairs by himself. Carrying anyone or making multiple trips wasn't going to happen.

Seth spotted a fire alarm pull on the wall of the darkened corridor. The building still had electricity to run the monitors, even though most of the overhead lights appeared to be burned out. That meant the odds were good the alarm still had power—and would go straight to the fire department.

He pulled the handle and winced as the sirens whooped, shattering the silence.

The trick is to get help for everyone else without getting caught myself. I've got work to do.

Seth moved as quickly as he could, keeping a hand on the grimy walls to steady himself. He remembered writing a text to send to Evan about an abandoned rehabilitation facility right before he got grabbed at the library. That told him where he was—and he'd figure out how to get back to Evan.

Why isn't Evan here? I thought he was real in the tunnel. Did I imagine everything—even the rescue?

Desperation flooded him with adrenaline. Searching for the steps to the ground floor led him to another locked door. Magic opened it faster than a lockpick. He made it down the stairs by hanging onto the railing the whole way, unsure when his legs might give out on him.

Seth stumbled to the door and cracked it open to see the parking lot. Overhead lights flickered disconcertingly in the twilight, barely illuminating the expanse of cracked asphalt, but he spotted a couple of large, armed men near the far corner of the building.

There's nowhere for me to run that they can't catch me.

Seth remembered the blueprints he had been looking at in the library, and how the hospital sat adjacent to the abandoned subway station.

It's a long shot, but if Osborn owns this building, he might have built an entrance to the old subway from the basement. I'd rather take my chances down there than fight my way past his goons.

While he had a signal, Seth dialed 911 on the stolen cell phone. "The people who've gone missing are in the old rehab hospital where the fire alarm just went off," he told the dispatcher. "Second floor, end of the hallway."

He had no idea where Evan was and worried since his boyfriend hadn't been the one to free him. Hoping that Evan wasn't in trouble of his own, Seth texted him with what he had realized in the dream-zone.

Unknown: *Got loose, heading for the tunnel. Osborn's amulet is his ring with the red stone. Be safe. Love you. - Seth*

He knew Evan's number by heart, but not Joe's, or Seth would have texted their new ally as well. His heart sank when an alert popped up indicating the message had failed to send.

Gonna have to hope Evan is okay and that he still gets the message. It's the best I can do for now.

Seth stumbled and caught himself. *Fuck. I'm barely staying on my feet, and I've got a long way to go.*

He used the phone's light to guide him down the stairs to the basement. Even if the electricity still worked, he didn't want to broadcast his location by turning on the overhead bulbs. Recalling what he'd seen on the floor plans, Seth headed toward the part of the cellar that would be closest to the old tunnel. *Let's hope I didn't just trap myself in a dead end.*

The fire klaxon reverberated in the concrete basement, making Seth's head throb. He knew he was in no shape to go up against Osborn and stop the ritual, but his worry that Evan might have been captured overruled caution.

He kept an eye out for anything he could use as a better weapon than the broken chair leg and spotted a heavy wrench discarded on a table. Seth ransacked a storage cabinet and found a faded and mildewed box of emergency candles and matches. He shoved as many of them as he could into his pockets and hefted the wrench.

Not as good as a machete or a battery-powered lantern, but I'll take what I can get.

Seth reached the back of the basement. He let the phone's light play over the wall, and his eyes widened when he saw a doorway that didn't look as old as the wall around it. The steel door's lock yielded to his spell, and Seth eased it open to reveal a dark void.

What did I expect? The tunnel hasn't been in use since the 1950s.

Seth gripped the wrench and lit a candle, hoping to save what remained of the phone's battery. He moved slowly down what seemed to be a side corridor and wished the candle illuminated more of his surroundings. *I can barely see two feet in front of me. But the light makes me a target for anyone—or anything—out there.*

When the corridor widened, Seth sighed in relief to see dim emergency lighting break the gloom. Once he reached the main tunnel, he blew out the candle and took a good look around.

"Subway" wasn't quite the right word, he thought. More like a tunnel to take streetcars under a section of bridge, back when trolleys ran on rails with an electrified overhead wire.

He had read articles about the yearly event that opened the station to the public, complete with a few of the old streetcars. Seth got his bearings, taking in the crumbling concrete, peeling paint, and places where mold blackened the plaster.

Time and neglect had not been kind to this place. Aside from that public event, the passageway remained unused—except, he suspected, by Osborn.

Three thousand feet of tunnel and two stations made up the subway. The "stations" hadn't been elaborate—just stairs from the sidewalk at street level leading to platforms with white-tiled walls. Those entrances had been locked long ago.

Getting out wasn't what worried Seth. Keeping Evan safe and stopping Osborn from going through with his ritual were the most important things.

Seth stayed close to the wall where the emergency lighting didn't quite reach, giving him scant cover in the shadows. He sniffed the still air, and amid the dust and mold, thought he smelled incense.

Osborn's here.

The date on the monitor was the day of the full moon. Seth had lost nearly four days of his life to Osborn's illusions, although in the dream, it seemed like weeks. He tamped down the grief over losing his family for a second time and focused on the danger at hand.

Was Osborn planning to come back to the old hospital and choose one of us to be his victim for the ritual? Since I ruined his plan, who is he going to use instead? Officer Nelson? Evan?

Seth's blood ran cold at the thought. *I've got to stop him without giving Osborn a third choice—me.*

He moved slowly and silently, canvassing the abandoned tunnel and landings for any additional weapons he could find. Yellowed newspapers and dried leaves piled in corners, and debris from the crumbling concrete arches littered the floor.

As he got closer, Seth heard a man's voice. He realized that Osborn probably had some of his goons with him. *Shit. It's bad enough to try to stop Osborn—but I'm not up to a fight.*

He wondered if Evan had been able to find the anchor. If Osborn was moving ahead with the ritual, either Evan hadn't managed to destroy the item yet, or the witch disciple was desperate enough to risk doing the ritual without it.

Osborn had claimed the old control room for his sacrifice—clever, Seth thought, The tours would have little reason to venture inside, so any overlooked evidence of the witch's activities were unlikely to be discovered.

He backed into a shadowed alcove as four bouncer-sized men emerged from the control room, jackets straining over muscles and shoulder holsters.

The subway had four possible entrances—five counting the secret door from the old hospital. The two stations for pedestrians and the entrance and exit for the trolley cars. The guards spread out, and Seth figured they were each taking an entrance.

If he had any chance of stopping the ritual, he had to size up the opposition. Seth waited until the men were out of sight, then he crossed the tracks, where he could move in the shadows. Since the electricity for the old trollies ran through an overhead wire, he didn't have to worry about a third rail. Seth tried not to think about rats, roaches, and other things that might lurk in the filth.

The guards didn't seem worried about interruptions. Seth had no idea where Evan and Joe were. *It's going to be one sorry rescue if it all comes down to me.*

He came to the east platform first. The guard leaned against the wall, oblivious to the stains that water and time had left on the cracked white tile. He didn't look up from his phone, thumbs flying, playing some sort of game. Seth moved noiselessly, staying in the darkest area against the far wall.

A man screamed in pain, and the sound echoed through the tunnel like something from a medieval dungeon. Seth shivered, praying that Evan wasn't the victim of whatever Osborn was doing.

Evan and Joe might not get here in time to save that poor bastard, even if they figure out where to go. I've got to do something.

Distract. Disrupt. Disarm. Seth had been a sniper in the Army, and while he didn't have his rifle, he hadn't forgotten his training.

He gathered some of the old paper and leaves together, trying hard not to think about spiders. Then he lit a match and set the bundle on fire, quickly moving to hide just beyond the glow in the darkness.

"What the hell?" the man yelled, looking up from his phone as the flames leaped high. "Fuck!" He headed to stomp out the fire.

Seth slipped behind him and brought the wrench down hard, dropping the guard without a sound.

He used the guard's belt to tie his wrists, knotted his shoestrings together, stuffed a dirty cloth in his mouth, then made certain that the fire was extinguished. Seth didn't envy the guard's headache when he woke.

One down — three and a witch to go.

Screams sounded again. Apparently, Osborn liked to toy with his victims. Torture hadn't been part of the other witch disciples' rituals, and several had drugged their sacrifices insensible. Seth pushed down his memories of nearly being offered up to Gremory's ghost himself and how close a thing it had been when he'd saved Evan.

Can't think about that now. I have a job to do. I'll deal with it later.

Seth moved along the tracks, careful to keep low. The next guard stood sentry at the closed trolley entrance. This time, Seth sent an empty metal can tumbling and clattering. The guard looked up then went back to his game. A flick of Seth's magic extended the can's roll, and the guard finally came to investigate. Seth lunged, pulling the guard off-balance, and the wrench knocked him cold.

After trussing him up like the first guard, Seth moved on, refusing to acknowledge the vertigo and headache that made it hard to walk a straight line.

From the control room, screams alternated with ragged breaths, and then a broken voice begged, "Please...please, no more."

Seth gritted his teeth, knowing he had to clear the guards before he could hope to intervene. Even then, going up against a full witch was suicide. He found a broken piece of rebar and welcomed having a second weapon.

If I were at my best and Osborn was as damaged as we've heard, I might get a lucky break. As it is, I've got a wrench, rebar, candles, and a bad attitude.

A combination of fire and a rattling worked to lure the third guard into a trap. But when Seth approached the west end of the tunnel, the fourth guard was missing, and the metal door was partially open.

10

EVAN

"WE'VE GOT A COMPLICATION," JOE SAID. EVAN AND JOHNNY LOOKED UP from where they were checking their weapons and spell components. They had claimed one of the gambling rooms at the speakeasy for their own, where no one was going to disturb them.

"Yeah? Like what?" Johnny asked. Despite a bag of items to work magic, he made sure the clip in his gun was full.

"Officer Nelson is missing," Joe replied. "I hacked into the internal police systems and set alerts for certain notifications," he told Evan. "It's a helpful way to know what's going on."

"You think Osborn did it? Took him?" Evan questioned.

Joe shrugged. "With Nelson's sparkling personality, I'm sure plenty of people want to get rid of him. But I also found notes from an Internal Affairs investigation—turns out Nelson is one of the few honest cops in Cleveland."

"He's still a dick," Johnny muttered.

"But he's not dirty. Considering the number of public officials Osborn's paid off over the years, that's commendable," Joe replied.

"Guess we've got to save him then." Evan gave an exaggerated sigh. He'd been twitchy since they'd started to get ready for the night's work. He really wanted to be part of the group headed for the old rehab hospital. Evan knew Jenna's team was best-suited for the job and could deal with interference from the police.

But his heart told him to go after Seth and to hell with the consequences.

"Osborn's desperate," Johnny said. "He needs the drugs to function with his injuries, but it's not enough anymore. He's got to tap the energy of more distant descendants in between the big rituals. But when you and Seth came looking for him, that forced his hand. He can't do without—and he's afraid that the two of you might take away his most valuable power boost—Nelson."

"Osborn likely had someone grab Nelson, gambling that sacrificing him earlier than his twelve-year cycle will still be a better recharge than what he could get from secondary descendants," Evan finished. "And then he'll deal with Seth and me."

Johnny nodded. "That's my theory—and I think it's valid. Just remember—there's nothing more dangerous than a cornered animal."

Evan finished checking his weapons and wandered over to stare at an old framed Pernod poster from the 1920s. He knew he needed to get his jittery thoughts under control or else he'd be a liability for the night's work.

Hang in there, Seth. We're coming for you.

"I'm not worried about Osborn being a stronger witch than I am," Johnny told Joe. "But he's ruthless, and now he's scared and feels backed into a corner. This is going to be a no-holds-barred fight. Just so you know."

Joe shrugged and shoved the machete he'd been sharpening into a sheath on his belt. "Kinda figured that."

Joe and Johnny combined their magic to open and then destroy Osborn's anchor. The contents were a hodgepodge of items—bones, an antique apothecary's measure, and some old charms that held dark resonance. The relative ease with which Joe and Johnny burned the items explained why keeping it hidden and bespelled had been so important to Osborn.

"The anchor's destroyed—Osborn's got to have felt that," Evan said. "His power reserve is gone. We've just got to stop him before he levels up with another hit from Gremory." He handed out the small cameras and earpieces Parker had created.

"Parker should be able to see the feed from all our cameras," he told them. "If we get separated, he can talk us through it." Evan held up another tiny camera mounted on a selfie stick. "We've also got this for looking around corners. It won't work in the pitch dark, but it beats sticking our necks out."

"I'm all for not making a target of ourselves. Let's get moving." Joe headed out the door with Evan right behind him and Johnny bringing up the rear.

When they reached the west trolley entrance, Johnny's magic opened the padlock on the access door next to the blocked tunnel entrance, easing it open soundlessly.

Evan used the camera stick, relieved to find the emergency lights kept the tunnel from complete darkness.

"There's a guard about twenty feet from your location," Parker reported through the comm link. "He doesn't seem to be paying a lot of attention."

Joe led the way inside, sticking to the shadows. Since he was protected by his patron Krukis's magic and unable to die by anything except the heat of a blast furnace, he'd "plow the road" and get rid of the guards.

Evan followed behind him, armed with a gun and a large knife. He didn't have the level of special abilities that either of his companions did, but he'd get the sacrifice victim to safety. Johnny brought up the rear, primed to use his magic against Osborn and stop the witch disciple's century-long murder spree.

The old subway's emergency lighting barely pierced the darkness. Glitchy overhead fixtures flickered, giving the passage a horror movie vibe. Joe dropped the guard with a punch, a burly goon who never had the chance to pull his gun.

They had guessed that the control room was the most likely place for Osborn's ritual. A man's screams broke the silence and echoed down the tunnel, proving their assumption right. Light glowed from the doorway.

"Shit—something's moving in the shadows," Parker warned. "Whatever it is, it's fast and weird."

The darkness seemed to come alive, and too late Evan remembered that Osborn's alliances weren't limited to mortals.

Two men slipped out of the control room and onto the platform with mesmerizing grace, while another pair climbed down head-first from the ceiling. In the dim light, their skin looked too pale, their eyes too bright.

Fuck. Vampires.

"Stay behind us," Joe snapped, moving toward the pair on the right as Johnny shifted to the left. The vamps came at Joe in a blur. One went for his throat, while the other grabbed an arm, going for the artery only to recoil when Joe's steel skin didn't pierce like human flesh.

"Break a fang?" Joe taunted as he closed his meaty fists around their necks and snapped them with a twist.

On the left, Johnny held out one hand, freezing the other two vampires in place with magic. Then he snapped his fingers and set them on fire.

Evan took a step back, realizing on a gut level just how out of his element he was. A new vampire rose right in front of him, lips drawn back and teeth bared.

He swung his machete, but the vamp easily dodged the blade. Before he could swing again, the creature gasped and arched as a piece of rebar stabbed him from behind. The vampire slumped, and Evan saw Seth holding the rebar, haggard and covered in black blood. Evan thought he was the most beautiful thing he'd ever seen.

"What the fuck!" Parker yelped into the comm link.

"There were three human guards farther down the track. I took care of them," Seth told them.

"How did you get here?" Evan could hardly believe that Seth was alive and with them.

Seth shook his head. "Later. I'm just glad I made it to the party."

Seth didn't look well, but he was on his feet and fighting—and alive. Evan figured that if they lived through tonight, everything else could be fixed.

Screams tore through the tunnel again, desperate and fading.

"Time to move," Joe growled. "Keep an eye out—there might be more surprises."

"Parker—time to go radio silent," Evan ordered. "You might not want to watch."

"Screw that. I've got your backs," Parker snapped and silenced the link.

Evan and Seth let Joe and Johnny lead the way, watching to make sure no new threats rose from the darkness. Evan kept stealing glances at Seth to make sure he was there.

"Fuck, he's started the ritual," Evan muttered as the light from inside the control room changed from the glow of fluorescent lights to the violet hue of magic.

Joe barreled through the doorway, sending the remaining guard inside the room sprawling with a roundhouse punch.

Derek Nelson lay stripped and bloody on a table in the middle of the old control room. Deep cuts gouged his chest and arms, and the glazed look in his eyes suggested that he was either drugged or going into shock.

"Help me," he groaned, his voice ravaged from screaming.

Behind him, Willis Osborn greeted them with a triumphant grin. "You're just in time for the main event." Blood spattered his white shirt and painted his forearms to the elbow.

An iridescent scrim of energy separated them from Osborn and Nelson, a magical curtain designed to keep anyone from interfering. Behind Osborn, a pinprick of violet light told Evan that despite them breaking Osborn's anchor, the witch disciple had siphoned enough energy from his captives to start the ritual and summon the trapped ghost of his old master.

Johnny blasted the energy curtain with a stream of glowing power. The transparent barrier held, growing brighter as it fought the attack.

Maintaining the scrim cost Osborn energy, so strengthening it against Johnny's barrage would drain the witch disciple. Evan knew from experience that shooting at the barrier or hitting it with an object would cause a potentially deadly rebound.

Joe stepped forward and pressed both open palms against the

barrier, making it spark and sizzle as his patron's power protected him from Osborn's magic.

Osborn raised both hands, palms out, and the barrier glowed more brightly when he sent his energy into the scrim. Evan feared that fending them off wouldn't stop the warlock from opening the rift to Gremory's trapped spirit.

Nelson lay still, no longer calling out for help.

Evan spotted the ornate garnet ring on the witch's right hand and tightened his grip on the machete, poised to spring. He spared a worried glance at Seth, who stood beside him shoulder-to-shoulder, still holding the wrench and rebar. *Seth looks like he might fall down at any moment. If he does, how can I get both Nelson and Seth to safety?*

The barrier flickered like the overhead lights, and Evan could see the strain in Osborn's face. Where Joe's hands touched the scrim, the barrier glitched.

"Get ready," Seth murmured, tensing to strike.

Nelson jerked upright and twisted, throwing himself on top of Osborn and taking them both to the floor.

The barrier flashed and vanished, but the purple rift grew larger, as if Gremory would not be denied his offering once summoned.

Osborn howled and struggled to throw Nelson off him as he stood to meet the new threat. Seth swung the wrench at the witch's head, and Osborn ducked, planting his hands on the table to steady himself. Nelson wrapped his arms around Osborn's knees, holding him in place as Evan brought the machete down on the witch's right wrist and severed his ring hand.

Osborn shrieked in pain. He fixed Evan with a murderous glare and raised his left hand, speaking the words of a spell. Seth grabbed the severed hand, ring and all, and threw it into the gaping purple rift that throbbed like a wound. The ring and hand vanished inside, and the violet light flared.

"Get out of there!" Johnny's shout jarred Evan into motion.

Osborn screamed as tendrils of light snaked from the rift and wrapped around his body, keeping him from finishing the spell.

Evan grabbed Nelson by the arm and yanked him to his feet. "Come on!"

Evan and Seth half-carried, half-dragged Nelson, desperate to put distance between themselves and Osborn.

"Go!" Johnny ordered.

Nelson could barely keep his feet, even supported by both Seth and Evan. Joe shoved them through the door with Johnny right behind him.

Evan looked over his shoulder and saw Osborn flailing as Gremory's power pulled him toward the rift. Osborn screamed again, pained and terrified as the rift claimed him, then vanished.

Out in the tunnel, Nelson sank to his knees. Seth and Evan stayed on guard while Joe and Johnny checked for other attackers, human or otherwise.

"What a mess," Evan murmured.

The bodies of the dead vampires littered the tracks, and the white tile walls were painted with blood. Evan thought the guards were still alive but had no idea what to do with them.

He turned to Joe and Johnny as they strode toward them. "We need to get Seth and Nelson to a hospital."

"Do you want to answer questions? Because I sure don't," Joe replied. "Jenna's got someone who can patch them up without drawing the wrong kind of attention. Her people can handle the clean-up too." He looked around the bloody station and grimaced.

"Let's get out of here." Joe wrapped his coat around Nelson, then scooped the cop into his arms as if he weighed nothing and led the way back to their cars. Evan got under Seth's shoulder and slipped an arm around his waist, but Seth managed the walk to the truck.

Joe deposited Nelson into the back seat of Seth's truck and pulled out his phone. "Hey Jenna—we need a medic and a clean-up crew. Yeah, the problem is handled, but we left a mess." He listened for a moment. "Okay. We'll be there. Thanks."

Joe turned back to the others. "Jenna said to bring them to room 36 at the Byway Inn. She'll have a medic meet us there."

"What about the old hospital? Did Jenna's team find any of the missing people? Are they okay?" Evan asked, and Seth's head snapped up.

"I'll tell you everything at the motel. Let's get out of here," Joe ordered.

Evan slid behind the wheel of the truck, and Seth climbed into the passenger seat without protest. The comm link crackled to life in his ear.

"Evan? Holy shit! What the fuck was that?" Parker sounded terrified and impressed all at once.

"That…was what we do," Evan replied. "I'll fill you in when we get back, but Seth and the cop are hurt, and we've got to meet up with a sketchy doctor to patch them up. Can you manage if we don't come home tonight?"

"Yeah, I'm good," Parker assured him. "I'm going to lock myself in the bedroom, sleep with the light on, and put one of your guns under my pillow, but I'll manage."

"Good. I'll pay for your therapy," Evan replied, only half-teasing. "Don't go out, don't let anyone in, and stay away from the windows."

"Yes, Mom," Parker snarked, and the link went silent again.

"Looks like I missed a lot," Seth said, eyeing the earpiece and the small improvised camera clipped to Evan's coat.

"Parker is our new tech wizard. He wants to be part of the team," Evan replied. "I think you'll like him."

"I woke up at the abandoned rehab hospital," Seth said as Evan drove away from the tunnel, with Joe and Johnny in the next car behind them. Nelson sat quietly in the backseat, and Seth handed him a bottle of water from the bin they kept beneath the front seat.

"Drink. It'll help with the shock. We'll get you patched up," Seth told the cop, who still looked dazed. "And get you some clothes and food."

"Drink some yourself—the doc is gonna fix both of you," Evan ordered.

Seth stayed in the truck with Nelson while Evan—who was less bloodstained—opened the door to the hotel room with a spell since they didn't have the key. Evan kept lookout while Seth hurried the bloody, nearly naked man into the room, then quickly closed the blinds before turning on a light.

"Do you need to use the restroom?" Evan asked, worried at how quiet the usually bombastic cop had become. He dug into the emergency kit he kept in the truck and set out a couple of bottles of water, protein bars, a spare T-shirt, and a pair of sweatpants.

"I can't promise the clothes will fit, but they're better than nothing," he said, handing off the items. Nelson nodded his thanks and stumbled into the bathroom, closing the door behind him.

Evan turned to Seth, and for the first time since his kidnapping, they were alone. "Come here," Evan said in a broken voice. Seth moved wordlessly into Evan's arms, hugging him so tight it was hard to breathe.

"I was scared," Evan confessed, burying his face in Seth's neck. Seth smelled of blood and sweat from days without a shower, which didn't bother Evan at all. Seth was alive, and he was here with him.

Evan kissed him, a gentle press against dry lips. Now wasn't the time for more, and Seth had his own recovering to do, but Evan ached to wrap his body around Seth and never let him go.

"So was I," Seth admitted. Evan felt Seth tremble and realized he hadn't gotten a good look at his injuries.

"The doc is going to take care of you too," Evan promised. He stepped back, giving Seth a head-to-toe scan. He saw bruising on Seth's hand from an IV, reddened skin around his wrists from cuffs, shadowed eyes, and a pallor that hadn't been there before.

"I pulled the fire alarm," Seth told him. "And I called 911 from the cell phone I stole to get someone there to rescue the others. They were in worse shape. Texted you, too."

Evan's heart dropped. "Shit. I didn't get a text—"

"It failed. Probably come through later." Seth gave a ragged laugh.

"We figured you and the others were at the old hospital, so Jenna took her Supernatural Secret Service team to bust you all out while we went after Osborn," Evan told Seth, leading him over to sit on the end of a bed.

Evan offered Seth a drink and food, but Seth shook his head. "Too much adrenaline in my system right now. I'd bring it all back up."

"I'm so sorry I wasn't with you at the library. If I had been—"

Seth turned to him and cupped Evan's face with one hand. "—they'd have taken you too. They drugged me, then used magic. It wasn't a fair fight. The only thing I could think of when I woke up was that you might have gotten away, that you were safe."

"Do you remember anything?"

Seth looked away, and Evan knew there was something he wasn't saying, something important. "I'll tell you later." Seth's tone warned Evan that whatever happened had been really bad.

"Whenever you're ready," Evan told him and kissed his temple. Seth managed a grateful smile in return.

Nelson emerged from the bathroom, shaky and shirtless but less bloody. He stumbled toward the other bed and fell more than sat. "Figured there was no point putting on a shirt while I'm still bleeding."

"Probably true," Evan replied, unsure how to react to this new side of the cop.

"Thanks for getting me out of there." Nelson went on without making eye contact. "I thought I was a goner. I still don't know how they got the drop on me."

Evan and Seth exchanged a look. "Drugs and magic," Seth replied. "That's how they got me too."

Nelson let out a sharp, harsh chuckle. "You tried to warn me."

"Someone primed you to mistrust us from the beginning," Evan said. "I'm betting that person has ties to Osborn. He played you to keep you from being protected."

"Yeah, I get that—now." Nelson sighed, wincing. The numerous cuts looked deep and had to hurt. "I knew that my family was 'unlucky.' We called it the 'Nelson curse.' My aunt thought some ancestor made a deal with the devil."

Seth shook his head. "No demon deal involved."

Nelson looked from Seth to Evan, all of his bluster gone. "You lost people too? That's why you do this?" Battered as he was, Nelson had moved into cop mode, and Evan wondered if it gave him a sense of control and a way to not freak out.

"Seth lost his brother. I lost my uncle—and would have been the next victim," Evan replied, sparing Seth the effort.

"There was one dark warlock—Gremory—whose spirit was trapped beyond that purple light. Sacrificing the descendants of the posse that killed him lets the warlock's disciples gain power and keeps

Gremory trapped, while sending enough energy through to the warlock to sustain him. So—twelve serial killer witches, committing ritual murders for a century." Evan put it in terms he knew Nelson's cop side would understand.

Nelson opened his mouth to say something, but just then, Jenna came through the door with an older man right behind her.

"Sorry it took us a bit—Mort lives a little way out of town." She nodded toward the stranger. "This is Mort Hudson—he's a retired Army doctor, and he works with the SSS for injuries that don't need to become public knowledge."

"Let's have a look. Agent Anderson has briefed me on the situation," Mort said, stepping forward.

Jenna turned to Evan. "I've put two undercover agents outside the room since you'll be staying the night." Her tone left no room for disagreement. "Mort will decide when you're cleared to leave. I'm claiming jurisdiction as of yesterday."

"Thank you," Evan told her. "That saves me the effort of arguing with them."

Seth glared, and Evan pointedly ignored him. Nelson didn't look well enough to protest.

Mort started with Nelson. Either the cop's earlier bluster was an act, or the trauma of the past few days had mellowed him. Evan found himself glad to discover that Nelson wasn't quite as big a douche as he first thought.

"You're dehydrated and depleted," Mort said when he finished his examination and then stitched and treated the cuts on Nelson's chest and arms. "And you've been through a traumatic experience. You need rest, liquids, food, antibiotics for those cuts, and dreamless sleep. Don't fuck with me. I'm the doctor."

He turned his attention to Seth, who reluctantly submitted to his examination. "You're the same—only more so. Are you always anemic? Eat, sleep, take it easy, drink a lot of water, lay off the booze, and go see a trauma therapist—but don't tell them the whole truth."

He left them with instructions on Nelson's dressings, plenty of sleeping pills, painkillers, and antibiotics, with a stern warning to rest.

Jenna walked Mort to the parking lot, leaving Seth, Evan, and Nelson alone.

"Looks like we're here for the night," Evan said. "I'll order pizza delivery and a couple of two-liters. Which you will drink," he said, mock-sternly with a glare aimed at both men. To his surprise, they didn't argue.

That told Evan that Seth and Nelson felt even worse than he thought.

They crashed early, not long after eating. Nelson was asleep in minutes. Seth and Evan weren't awake much longer. Evan made sure Seth took the pills Mort had left for him, then they crawled into bed, exhausted.

Seth rolled next to Evan so that they were touching from shoulders to ankles. "I need the contact," he murmured. "Need to know you're really here with me."

Evan gave him a look at the odd way Seth phrased that, wondering if there was a deeper meaning.

"I'm here. Not going anywhere," Evan assured him. "Sleep—I'll keep you safe."

Seth sighed and closed his eyes. Minutes later, Evan heard his breathing change and knew the pills had done their job. *Here's hoping both of them make it through the night without bad dreams.* Evan wished he could guarantee the same for himself.

IN THE MORNING, A KNOCK AT THE DOOR HAD EVAN REACHING FOR his gun.

"Don't shoot—I brought donuts," Jenna called out, and Evan forced himself to relax. He hadn't slept soundly, hypervigilant for any sound of distress from Seth or Nelson.

Evan let Jenna in and saw that she had large cups of coffee in addition to a bag of donuts. She set the food on the table and took a seat, so Evan guessed breakfast was the bribe to hear what the agent had to say.

"Seth's in the shower," Evan fetched a donut and coffee for Nelson, then a coffee for himself, and sat on the end of the bed. "Thanks for this. I thought I'd need to forage."

Seth sauntered out of the bathroom, looking better after a night's sleep and a hot shower. Someone who didn't know him might not have seen the signs of strain Evan saw immediately in the line of his jaw and the darkness in his eyes. He headed straight for the donuts, swiping a Boston Creme and a coffee before sitting next to Evan, pressed together from knee to hip.

"I'm guessing breakfast comes with strings attached," Seth said, wary.

Evan knew Seth hadn't met Jenna before the battle and didn't have Joe's endorsement to vouch for her.

Jenna smiled. "Not exactly—but I'd appreciate it if you'd hear me out."

"I'm a cop. You had me at 'donuts.'" Nelson took a bite that covered his chin with powdered sugar.

"What do you plan to do now?" Jenna asked Nelson. "Before you answer, let me say that Osborn has been watched for a while now by the Supernatural Secret Service for everything from illegal pharmaceuticals to trafficking people with special abilities. He got away with a lot because he had friends in high places and paid off the right cops."

Nelson stilled and looked away.

"Word on the street says you're an honest cop," Jenna continued. "Can't have been easy. Going back might not be ideal if Osborn's cronies link you to his 'disappearance.'"

"What's the spin going to be on that?" Seth asked. "Tax evasion? Cartel hit? Securities fraud?"

Jenna shrugged. "Still working on that. Probably a storyline that puts his accomplices and collaborators on notice. He's not the only kingpin, unfortunately."

She turned back to Nelson. "We're going after the dirty cops who turned a blind eye to Osborn's dealings all these years. It could get... uncomfortable...at headquarters. On the other hand, our agency is always looking for good people."

Nelson raised his head; surprise clear on his face. "I think I'd like to hear more about that once I catch my breath."

She laid a business card on the table. "Contact me when you're ready. We'll talk." Jenna turned toward Seth and Evan.

"I know better than to try to recruit you—you're not the type. But we can be allies. You don't have to do this completely on your own," Jenna told them. Evan's respect for the agent rose at not getting a hard sell.

"We'll think about it," Evan said, "depending on the situation."

She handed Evan a card as well. "If you lose the card, Joe can usually find me. We seem to run in the same circles."

With that, Jenna rose and headed for the door. "You've got the security detail through tonight. Mort will be by later to check on you. My team will clear out tomorrow morning, and I can't vouch for who might show up after us, so you may want to plan accordingly."

"Thanks," Seth said, and Evan nodded his agreement.

"Always happy to help," Jenna replied, closing the door behind her.

"How are you doing?" Evan asked Nelson, not sure what kind of answer he'd get.

"Frankly? It's all a bit much to take in," Nelson admitted.

Now that he'd dropped his bluster, he didn't seem like a bad guy. Evan was willing to give Nelson a second chance. Seth looked skeptical, but didn't say anything.

"I went on the run with Seth four days after we met when he saved me from the Richmond witch disciple," Evan said. "I didn't entirely believe him at first, either. I'd heard about the family 'bad luck,' but not the real reasons for it. It took a while to wrap my head around what Seth told me. Once you know, there's no way to go back."

"Kinda figured that," Nelson said. He took a long gulp of coffee. "Guess I've got some decisions to make."

Evan made sure Seth and Nelson had everything they needed, then stepped outside to call Parker and reassure his panicking brother that they had survived and were coming back. He saw Mort, the doctor, pull up in his truck.

"Things go okay last night?" Mort asked. "They sleep good?"

Evan nodded. "I was worried, but neither of them had nightmares —at least for now."

"Those will come," Mort warned. "Sooner or later. It's the brain's way of dealing with trauma."

"Not the first rodeo for either of us with that," Evan said. "We'll manage."

He brought the doc inside. Seth and Nelson grudgingly went along with being poked and prodded. Mort checked wounds for infection, changed the dressings, and repeated his instructions for the painkillers and antibiotics.

"I think I've done all I can." He packed his bag to leave. "Take care of yourselves. Try not to undo all my hard work."

When Mort had gone, Seth looked to Evan. "Now what?"

Evan tossed him the remote. "Now, you two rest. Find a movie or watch a game. Sleep. I'll order sub sandwiches for lunch, and you can eat when you're hungry."

"What about you?" Seth looked petulant.

"I didn't get whammied and tortured, so even though I got shitty sleep, I'm in somewhat better shape," Evan replied, raising an eyebrow. "I have some books on my phone. Might be persuaded to take a nap if you're nice to me," he added with a grin.

Seth sighed as if he knew when he'd lost. He glanced at Nelson. "You want to pick?" he asked, holding up the remote.

Nelson shook his head. "Don't care. I'll probably be out again as soon as I lie down."

Once the cop settled into his bed, Evan came over and propped his pillows against the headboard so he could sit next to Seth. "Figured I'd read while you watch TV," he said, reassuring himself with a glance that Seth was alive and here.

"I like that plan," Seth said with a tired smile. He yawned, and Evan wondered how far Seth would make it before he fell asleep. Half an hour into the movie, Seth had drifted off, sliding to one side and resting his head on Evan's shoulder.

Evan closed his eyes, leaned his cheek against Seth's hair, and said a silent thank-you to the universe for deliverance.

11

SETH

EARLY THE NEXT MORNING, EVAN HAD BARELY PARKED THE TRUCK BEFORE the RV's door slammed open, and a man Seth didn't know ran out, plowing into Evan and nearly knocking him off his feet before wrapping him in a bear hug.

"Oh, my God, Evan! Are you okay? Are you hurt? The video cut out, and I didn't get to see what happened."

"Seth, this is my brother, Parker," Evan managed in a strangled tone. "Parker, meet Seth. The only reason you aren't flat on your ass with a knife at your throat for jumping me is that he's feeling a little under the weather."

Parker let go and stepped back, casting a nervous glance at Seth, who had moved forward protectively with a dangerous scowl. "Um, hi. I'm Evan's little brother. Glad you're both back safe."

Evan clapped a hand on Parker's shoulder. "The cameras gave us an important heads up, but they're fragile in a fight. Something to work on for next time."

Evan and Seth followed Parker back into the RV. Everything was right again—the photos of him and Evan, the dish towels in the kitchen, the gun in the drawer, and—he was sure if he went to check— the lube in the nightstand. All the things he had missed in the hallucination that Osborn's magic used to pacify him while his life drained away.

Mom, Dad, Jesse—they weren't real. So why do I miss them so much?

"Hey, you okay?" Evan asked, and Seth realized he had zoned out.

He nodded, fighting back tears. "Yeah. Just a little spacey from everything. I'll be fine."

The glint in Evan's eyes told Seth that his boyfriend read the lie for what it was.

Evan looked at the mess of spare parts strewn across the table. "What's that?"

Parker grinned. "Already working on a way to make the cameras more durable and fasten them better. And that—" he pointed to a small heap, "is going to be a drone you can send in before risking your neck." He shrugged. "I had to do something after I lost the video feed because I was climbing the walls."

Evan turned to Seth. "Parker is a whiz-kid engineer. He rigged up battle cams for us so he could watch and relay info with comm links. They got broken, but it was a good first try." Parker glowed at his big brother's approval.

Engineer. Jesse was going to be an engineer. Another wave of grief hit Seth.

"Parker wants to be our gadget guy," Evan continued. He looked happy, not just relieved, and after his own "reunion" with Jesse, Seth understood. "He can come up with high-tech stuff that keeps us from getting killed. Around his classes and job, of course," Evan added.

"About that—" Parker went into the kitchen and filled coffee cups for Seth and Evan, then refilled his own. "I don't want to go back to Columbus. I want to stay in Cleveland. Now that I know there are *things* out there in the dark, I feel safer with your friends around."

"Thanks for sparing me an awkward conversation where I was going to try to convince you to do that," Evan chuckled.

"And I'm not going back to Oklahoma to visit," Parker added, with a defiant and resolute expression. "I had a lot of time to think while you were gone. Nothing's changed with Dad. Once you left, he found things to pick at me about. I'm sorry he's sick, but he's got Mom, Jim, good insurance, and money to hire help if they need it. I'll just be a piñata if I go home, and so would you. We don't owe him that."

Evan looked proud. "We can do a video call if we need to—assuming he'd even accept the invitation. Let's worry about that later."

Watching Evan and Parker together made the ache worse in Seth's chest. As glad as he was that Evan and his brother had reforged their bond, Jesse was lost to him forever.

Evan's phone rang. "Hey, Joe. We're safely back home. Everything okay? I'm putting you on speaker."

"Just checking in. Jenna gave me her side of things, but I like to hear it from the source," Joe rumbled.

"I'm fine, Seth is doing better, and Parker has some second-generation gadget ideas you'll want to see," Evan replied. "You and Johnny okay? I was so busy with Seth and Nelson I forgot to ask."

Seth was content to let Evan do the talking. He hadn't met Joe or Johnny before the battle, although he knew the names. Evan had called in the cavalry, and Seth felt proud of how far he'd come in barely a year of hunting.

"Yeah, we're kinda hard to kill," Joe said. "Jenna's people cleaned up the mess, so there shouldn't be awkward questions. She's whisked Nelson off to some kind of paranormal WITSEC, and between the information Adrian's data mining turned up and Jenna's intel, it looks like Osborn's drug empire will get shut down permanently."

"That's a nice bonus," Evan agreed. "Hey, I've got a favor to ask. Parker wants to stay in Cleveland. Can you make some suggestions?"

"Sure. I can help him get settled. After all, I've been here for more than a century," Joe said, and Seth could hear the smile in his voice.

"Thanks. I'll give him your number."

Seth looked up as Evan ended the call. "I'm going to go lie down," he said, not sure he could hold his composure much longer as the memories of Jesse and his family came flooding back.

Evan nodded, his expression hard to read. "Sure. You need the rest. Mort said it would take a while to rebound."

Seth felt like he was running away, but he couldn't muster the energy to face the feelings that threatened to drag him under.

Jesse's been dead for more than three years. I thought I'd accepted it. I guess not.

The time spent with the illusion had brought his ghosts to life. Seth knew he'd have to deal with them, but he hadn't been lying when he told Evan he was tired. Soul searching would have to wait. Just the short time he had been awake felt like it had drained him completely.

He fell asleep, tossing and turning, and his dreams were dark.

~

WHEN SETH WOKE, EVAN LAY BESIDE HIM. "YOU WERE RESTLESS. I thought it might help if you weren't alone."

Seth reached for Evan's hand and twined their fingers. "It's always better when you're here."

Evan pushed the hair from Seth's face and stroked fingertips down his cheek. "You know you can talk to me about anything, right? Whatever happened to you while you were gone—I'm here if you need to work through it."

Seth nodded. "I know. I'm just not ready yet." He squeezed Evan's hand. "But I will. Give me time."

Evan leaned down to kiss him. "As much time as you need. I'll be waiting."

The next time Seth woke, Evan was sound asleep beside him. Seth eased out of bed, knowing that Evan also needed to recover.

He slipped out of the bedroom and found Parker tinkering at the table.

Parker looked up. "Evan's been twisted up in knots about you."

Seth managed a chagrined smile. "Sorry about that. I'd have rather avoided the whole thing."

"I'm sure." Parker gave him an appraising look. "I think you're good for Evan. He cares about you a lot, so don't fuck it up."

"I will do my best to avoid that," Seth replied solemnly.

"Good. Because I'd be honor-bound to try to kick your ass, and I don't think I'd win."

Despite everything, Seth snorted a laugh. "Are all the Malones this feisty?"

Parker sobered. "Unfortunately not. Or we might have put an end to this murder stuff a long time ago. Evan has brass balls for going on a witch-killing rampage with you. Damn. I'm impressed."

"I know it means a lot to Evan that you're here," Seth said. "He missed you."

"We traded letters and emails, called each other sometimes," Parker said. "I took too long leaving home. I should have followed Evan's example a while ago. He's always been my hero."

Seth smiled, thinking of all the times Evan had his back. "Mine, too."

"Do you need something?" Parker asked. "Food? Drink? You're the one recovering."

Seth shook his head. "No, thank you. But my thoughts are still jumbled. I want to take a cup of coffee outside and just sit for a while. If Evan wakes up, please tell him where I am."

Parker pointed his finger at Seth. "You got it."

Seth took his coffee and grabbed a jacket as he slid into his boots. The late fall day was cold, and dark clouds promised snow.

He went out to the picnic table that was within the wards around the RV. The wood was warped and gray but still strong enough to bear his weight. *That's good, because I'm broken enough.*

Seth wrapped both hands around his steaming mug and perched on the table, resting his boots on the seat.

I'm mourning the memories of a dream. None of that really happened. Mom and Dad and Jesse are dead. Everything I thought I experienced was a lie.

His chest tightened, making it hard to breathe. *It was a lie—but I wanted it to be true. If Evan had been there, it would have been perfect.*

How do I let go? How do I mourn them a second time?

Seth set his cup aside. Then he bowed his head and wept so hard that his shoulders shook, and he gasped for breath. *I've lost them —again.*

He heard footsteps crunch on the dry grass and knew Evan had come looking for him. Seth didn't look up. He felt Evan settle next to him. For a while, they sat in silence while Evan drank the coffee he'd brought out with him.

Seth dragged his sleeve across his eyes, sniffing back the last of the tears. He still couldn't look at Evan without breaking down again, and he was grateful that Evan knew him well enough to give him space instead of hauling him into a hug right now.

"That bastard Osborn magicked me into a hallucination," Seth said finally. "I was home with Mom and Dad and Jesse just like when I first came back from the Army."

"Figured something like that," Evan murmured.

Seth stared into the distance. "I didn't remember the real world, except I knew we shouldn't go to the hell gate bridge. Jesse and I hung out. Mom and Dad were looking forward to retirement. Everything was good, except…"

Evan waited, letting Seth tell his story in his own time, and Seth appreciated his patience.

"Every now and then, I'd see things that no one else saw. My gun in a drawer. You in the crowd, over and over again," Seth said in a low, confessional tone. "I'd look at the RV and know it wasn't the way it should be, but I didn't know why. Then we went to Richmond, and I kept getting flashes of memories. We went to Treddy's, and I knew you should be there, but I didn't know why. Then I saw you and followed you, and you told me to run, that I didn't belong there."

When Evan stayed quiet, Seth went on. "Jesse helped me figure out what was going on, and he helped me get away. You…you came for me, and you led me through the Church Street Tunnel, and we had to fight monsters to come out the other side. That's when I woke up."

Seth reached over and took Evan's hand, silent permission for him to tell his part of the story.

"I searched for you," Evan finally said. "I called Milo and Toby when you vanished. One thing led to another, and I got referred to Joe. He brought in Jenna and Adrian, and Travis helped me crack the spell so Parker and I could steal the anchor. Then Johnny worked a spell that let me contact you. I'm sorry that it took me so long to figure it out. And that I wasn't the one to rescue you."

"You sent Jenna and her people to storm the old hospital. If I hadn't woken up and gotten out on my own, you would have saved me," Seth replied.

"Glad you were badass enough to save yourself."

"I was afraid Osborn grabbed you. What happened to Nelson was awful, but I'm glad it wasn't you."

"I still didn't know for sure where you were when I went into the subway with Joe and Johnny," Evan said. "And then you were there, rescuing me."

"Always."

They were quiet again for a while. Finally, Evan sighed and looked out into the distance. "I'm sorry that you had to lose Jesse and your folks. But I'm grateful that you came back to me."

Seth turned to Evan and turned him so that their eyes met. "All the time I was in the dream, you were what was missing. I can live without Jesse. I can't live without you."

Seth leaned in and kissed Evan.

"You ready to go back inside? It's cold out here. Plus, the sooner you recover, the sooner I can show you just how much I missed you," Evan replied with a glint in his eyes.

"I hope your brother is a sound sleeper."

12

EVAN

"You've got an apartment and a job to tide you over, and you've signed up for classes next term. Looks like you're all set." Evan slapped Parker on the back. They stood outside the building where, with the help of Joe's network of friends, Parker had found an affordable place in a neighborhood Joe assured them was safe.

Seth and Johnny had warded the apartment and as much of the common space as they could, leaving Parker with enough protective hex bags to keep him safe against routine magical threats. Evan could sleep easier now that he knew Joe, Johnny, and their friends were watching over his little brother. They understood he would be in danger until the last disciple was gone.

"I appreciate everything you've done," Parker said. "I promised Johnny I'll be the best bar back he's ever had. And you heard them; they won't let me slack off on college either."

"Just steer clear of the Laveccia family business, like Johnny usually does," Evan warned.

Parker nodded. "You have my word on it." He pulled Evan in for a hug.

Evan hugged him back. "And I promise to be better about staying in touch. In between monster hunts."

"You've got a gadget guy now, remember? Let me know what you need, and I'll figure out how to keep you safer."

"The gadgets could become a whole side business for you," Evan said. "There are a lot of hunters out there who don't have a knack for tech. You might be surprised at the possibilities."

"I just want to help, even from a distance," Parker told him. "Make sure you keep me in the loop."

"Be careful what you wish for," Evan told him, then headed for the truck where Seth was waiting and waved again as they drove away.

Neither of them said anything until they were outside of Cleveland. Evan was wrapped up in his thoughts, wishing Parker well and still worried about the aftereffects of Osborn's magic on Seth.

"I think your brother's an okay guy," Seth said finally. "He'll be better off in Cleveland than anywhere else since Joe will keep an eye on him."

Evan nodded. "I know, and I'm grateful. I just hoped we could settle all this without Parker ever needing to know about witches or magic or the things we hunt."

"He's safer this way."

Evan sighed. "And he'll never be able to look at the world the same way again." He shook his head. "I guess I can't quit being a big brother."

Seth's expression grew wistful. "Neither can I."

Evan sobered quickly, "I'm sorry—"

"Don't be." Seth reached for Evan's hand and laced their fingers together. "I've been thinking about the illusion...spending time with Jesse and my parents. I know Osborn meant it to keep me docile. I know it wasn't real. But...in a strange way, it filled a big hole."

Seth was quiet for a moment, and Evan guessed he was gathering his thoughts. "I never got to say goodbye to them," he said finally. "Not in the real world. Jesse and I were goofing around, and then all of a sudden, he was gone. We didn't get much time together after I came home from the Army. I could have had six more years with him if I hadn't been stupid and enlisted to run away from my mistakes."

He let out a long breath and swallowed hard. "My parents died in a car wreck while I was in the hospital. I didn't get to say goodbye to them, either. And then, for so long, I focused on the pain and the anger, and I forgot the good memories."

Evan stayed silent, waiting for Seth to find his words. "In a really weird way, Osborn gave that back to me. The memories from the illusion might not be 'real,' but they were 'true' because my brain invented them from things that might have happened. I have those 'memories' now, and they're good. While I'm sad Jesse and the others are gone, I feel like I got something I never dared to hope for —closure."

Silent tears rolled down Evan's face, and he swiped at them with his free hand. "I'm glad that you found a way to make something good out of all this."

"We're alive and together. Everything else can be fixed." Seth squeezed Evan's hand.

"Let's take some time off before we go to Savannah," Evan said suddenly. "I think we both need time to recover, not just throw ourselves into the next hunt."

Evan looked apprehensive until Seth smiled in response. "I think you're right," he said, relieved when Evan relaxed at his words. "We need a break. I think we've earned it."

"Where do you want to go?"

Evan shrugged. "Someplace quiet with a nice view."

Seth's phone rang. "That's Toby—we've been texting about Milo," he told Evan. Seth read the newest text and let out the breath he'd been holding. "Milo's doing better," he read aloud for Evan's sake. "Should be released tomorrow. Still grumpy as always."

"I'm glad he's okay," Evan replied.

"Me, too."

Over lunch, they searched for nearby open campgrounds that had both a great location and the amenities for a comfortable week-long stay. Seth found a good spot at a nearby year-round campground.

"It's quiet, with parking spots that look out onto the lake and absolutely no reported supernatural activity."

Evan grinned. "Perfect."

They stocked the RV's fridge before they left the Cleveland

suburbs, making sure they had everything they needed to stay at least a week—even if they got snowed in.

"This place is beautiful," Evan said as Seth took the long way to their campsite to get a look around. Ice verged a small lake, and while the mini-golf was closed for the winter, a sign on the campground canteen advertised sled and cross-country ski rentals.

"What do you want to do first?" Evan asked.

"Honestly? Cook a good meal, warm up and relax with a glass of scotch, turn on the fireplace and curl up with you on the couch. Movie optional."

"That sounds wonderful," Evan agreed. "I have some ideas about things to do if the movie doesn't hold your interest." He added a smile that promised a good time.

"I'm looking forward to taking you up on that proposition." Seth grinned. "I don't care if we leave the trailer—or the bed—for the rest of the week."

Lasagna with a salad and garlic bread made for a hearty meal and plenty of leftovers. Seth poured scotch for both of them, and they settled into the puffy leather couch facing the TV and the electric fireplace. Seth sat sideways so that Evan could nestle between his legs with his back against Seth's chest.

They sipped the whiskey and picked an action movie they had seen dozens of times before.

Evan closed his eyes and rested his head against Seth. He lifted Seth's arm so it was over his chest and breathed in his scent, reassuring himself that they were alive and together.

That first night, lecherous plans aside, both Seth and Evan fell asleep twined together on the couch from sheer exhaustion. Long after the movie ended, Seth roused Evan, and they stumbled to bed, still half-asleep.

In the morning, Evan awoke in Seth's arms. He lay still for a moment, listening to his lover breathe, overwhelmed and grateful to have him alive and back in his bed.

Evan's fingers traced lazily up and down Seth's chest. "Sleep well?"

Seth nodded. "I didn't dream. And I'm with you, so it's all good."

Evan felt Seth's cock stir. "What do you want?" Evan kissed Seth's bare chest. He shifted so he could rub against Seth's thigh.

"I want you to fuck me and remind me we're both alive," Seth murmured, letting his hand run up and down Evan's flank. "And when we're done, I'll return the favor."

"I'll never turn down an offer like that." Evan leaned in to lick at Seth's nipples until they pebbled beneath his tongue. He slid a hand down to tease Seth's cock through the sheet with slow strokes, alternating palm and fingertips until Seth gasped and arched, and a wet spot made his hunger clear.

"Evan," Seth groaned. "Need you."

Evan rolled on top of Seth, settling between his thighs. Evan tugged Seth's boxer-briefs down and managed to wriggle out of his own at the same time. They'd left clothing in a trail across the floor the night before.

Seth grabbed the lube from the nightstand drawer. "That was one of the ways I knew that I wasn't in the right place in the dream-world," he said. "No lube."

Evan squeezed out a measure of the gel, rubbing his palms together to warm it before he took both of them in hand with sure, smooth strokes. Seth's fingertips glided up and down Evan's back, then across the firm muscles of his shoulders and upper arms, and down to squeeze his ass. *Maybe he needs to reassure himself that this is real,* Evan thought.

"Want to come with you inside me," Seth breathed. "Want to feel you fill me up."

"Shh. I'm getting there." Evan twisted his hand over the heads of their cocks, intense enough that it nearly sent them both over the edge.

Evan let go and sat back on his haunches, using more lube to ease his finger into Seth's tight hole. Seth wriggled to urge him deeper, and Evan obliged, adding a second finger and then a third. He grazed Seth's sweet spot, sending shocks of pleasure through Seth's body.

"Please," Seth moaned. "I'm ready. Ready enough."

"Don't want to hurt you."

"You won't. I need an edge to it this time," Seth confessed. "To make it real. I want the burn. I want to feel you afterward all day, a reminder."

Evan regarded him for a moment, then nodded. "Okay." He hooked his elbows under Seth's thighs and pulled Seth toward him until they were aligned.

"This okay?" Evan pressed in, stilling as soon as he had breached the entrance.

"Better than okay." Seth reached down to palm Evan's ass and pull him closer. "Fuck me like you mean it."

"You know I do." Evan pressed deeper, one long stroke until he was balls-deep. He waited for a few seconds for Seth to adjust, then he gripped Seth's hips and began to thrust.

Given all the tension and emotions of the past few days, it took less time than usual to reach climax. Evan might have been embarrassed about how quickly he came, except that Seth orgasmed first with an intensity that had him biting his lip and wrapping his legs around Evan's waist to drive Evan's cock as deep as possible.

Evan followed seconds later, spilling inside his lover's tight channel, riding out the aftershocks eased by the slick of his come. He released his grip on Seth's hips and let his hands slide up Seth's chest, then leaned forward to kiss him.

"Best cure for whatever ails you," he whispered, peppering a string of kisses from Seth's jawline down to his collarbone.

Seth brought his arms up around Evan's back, pulling him into an embrace and splaying his large hands across Evan's bare back. "Round two is my turn."

"I like that plan," Evan replied, continuing to kiss his way down Seth's body, licking up all of the come that had pooled on Seth's abs, then following his happy trail to his cock, which was already beginning to plump once more.

Evan took all of Seth's softened dick into his mouth, caressing it with his lips and tongue as his hand gently rolled Seth's balls and then moved to tease at his sensitive, slick hole. Seth moaned, urging Evan on, and Evan used his weight on Seth's thighs to keep him from bucking and wriggling.

Seth's cock filled as Evan licked and sucked at the shaft and traced the broad head, sliding through the slit with the tip of his tongue.

Sooner than Evan expected, Seth was hard again, and Evan had all of him in his mouth, bumping at the back of his throat.

"Keep doing that, and I'm not going to last for the main event," Seth warned. "Go on—open yourself up. Let me watch."

Evan gave him a wicked grin. "I snuck off to the bathroom for a little prep before you woke up." He squirted some lube onto his hand and slicked Seth's stiff prick, then shifted forward on his knees, lining himself up and giving Seth a show as he took him all the way to the root.

"Oh God, Evan. So good," Seth managed, gripping the sheets in his fists as Evan rose and then dropped down again.

"Missed you. Missed this," Evan murmured, setting up a rhythm that assured neither of them would last long.

Seth squirted lube into his palm and stroked Evan's cock back to firmness, matching the pace. He smiled as Evan trembled and raced toward climax. Evan could tell that Seth was getting close again and knew how much it turned his lover on to see him fuck himself on Seth's cock.

"Christ, you're beautiful. Watching you do that is the sexiest thing ever," Seth breathed.

Evan moved his hips in a slow figure-eight, and Seth cried out, coming hard again. Evan came seconds later, clenching around Seth's cock, head thrown back, moaning as his whole body shook with the force of his climax.

Evan folded forward on top of Seth, still joined, and kissed him slow and careful.

"Think I know what they mean when they talk about 'coming your brains out,'" Seth said, stroking his clean hand through Evan's hair as Evan mouthed at his throat and sucked a hickey at the base of Seth's neck. "I can barely string words together. I think my vision whited out there for a bit."

"Good," Evan murmured. "S' what I was trying to do. Distract you."

Seth lightly stroked Evan's back with one hand as his other hand toyed with his hair. "Oh, I was plenty distracted. For the record—I'm a fan of waking up like that."

"Hmm. I'll keep that in mind," Evan joked, sounding sleepy and spent. He rolled away reluctantly, letting Seth slip out. "Guess I'd better wipe us up before we stick together."

He padded to the bathroom and returned with a warm towel to clean away the jizz from Seth's chest and pubes, wiping down his thighs and over his sensitive hole before washing himself as well. Evan tossed the cloth in the general direction of the bathroom and settled back beside Seth.

"You know we're going to need to eat, sooner or later," Seth said with a chuckle.

Evan's reply was a non-committal murmur as he nestled closer to Seth. "Sleep longer. Vacation."

Seth turned to press a kiss to Evan's temple, and Evan bit down on Seth's shoulder hard enough to leave the impressions of his teeth without breaking the skin. "Mine," Evan mumbled.

"All yours, Evan," Seth assured him. "Now and forever."

ACKNOWLEDGMENTS

Thank you so much to my editor, Jean Rabe, to my husband and writing partner Larry N. Martin for all his behind-the-scenes hard work, and to my wonderful cover artist Lou Harper. Thanks also to the Shadow Alliance and the Worlds of Morgan Brice street teams for their support and encouragement, and to my fantastic beta readers: Amy, Andrea, Carole, Christopher, Donald, Sandra, Scott, and Seth, plus my promotional crew and the ever-growing legion of ARC readers who help spread the word, including: Amanda, Anne, Ashley, Austin, Ben, Beth, Dawn B., Dawn R., Debbie, Diane, Galena, Hannah, Harrison, Jamie, Janet, Janneke, Jason, Jen, Jerri, Jessy, Kandice, Kendra, Kendra, Kimberly, Kitty, Kristen, Laurie, Manon, Mary, Rosalind, Sandy, Scott, Shakera, Sherrie, Shirley, Sue, Susan, Terri, Terry, Theresa, and more!

I couldn't do it without you! And of course, thanks and love to my "convention gang" of fellow authors for making road trips and virtual cons fun.

ABOUT THE AUTHOR

Morgan Brice is the romance pen name of bestselling author Gail Z. Martin. Morgan writes urban fantasy male/male paranormal romance, with plenty of action, adventure, and supernatural thrills to go with the happily ever after.

Gail writes epic fantasy and urban fantasy, and together with co-author hubby Larry N. Martin, steampunk and comedic horror, all of which have less romance and more explosions.

On the rare occasions Morgan isn't writing, she's either reading, cooking, or spoiling two very pampered dogs.

Watch for additional new series from Morgan Brice and more books in the Witchbane, Badlands, Treasure Trail, Kings of the Mountain, and Fox Hollow universes coming soon!

Where to find me, and how to stay in touch

Join my Worlds of Morgan Brice Facebook Group and get in on all the behind-the-scenes fun! My free reader group is the first to see cover reveals, learn tidbits about works-in-progress, have fun with exclusive contests and giveaways, find out about in-person get-togethers, and more! It's also where I find my beta readers, ARC readers, and launch team! Come join the party!

https://www.Facebook.com/groups/WorldsOfMorganBrice

Find me on the web at https://morganbrice.com. Sign up for my newsletter and never miss a new release! http://eepurl.com/dy_8oL. You can also find me on Twitter: @MorganBriceBook, on Pinterest (for Morgan and Gail): pinterest.com/Gzmartin, on Instagram as Morgan-BriceAuthor, on YouTube at https://www.youtube.com/c/GailZ-MartinAuthor/ and on Bookbub

https://www.bookbub.com/authors/morgan-brice
Enjoy two free short stories set in Fox Hollow: Nutty for You -
https://claims.prolificworks.com/free/r54nldjv
and Romp - https://claims.prolificworks.com/free/I4lCYKli
Check out the ongoing, online convention ConTinual www.facebook.com/groups/ConTinual

Support Indie Authors

When you support independent authors, you help influence what kind of books you'll see more of and what types of stories will be available, because the authors themselves decide which books to write, not a big publishing conglomerate. Independent authors are local creators, supporting their families with the books they produce. Thank you for supporting independent authors and small press fiction!

ALSO BY MORGAN BRICE

Badlands Series

Badlands

Restless Nights, a Badlands Short Story

Lucky Town, a Badlands Novella

The Rising

Cover Me, a Badlands Short Story

Loose Ends

Leap of Faith, a Badlands/Witchbane Novella

Night, a Badlands Short Story

No Surrender

Fox Hollow Zodiac Series

Huntsman

Again

Fox Hollow Universe

Romp, a Fox Hollow Novella

Nutty for You, a Fox Hollow Short Story

Imaginary Lover

Haven

Gruff

Trash and Treasure, a Fox Hollow Novella

Kings of the Mountain Series

Kings of the Mountain

The Christmas Spirit, a Kings of the Mountain Short Story

Treasure Trail Series

Treasure Trail

Blink

Light My Way Home, a Treasure Trail Novella

Witchbane Series

Witchbane

Burn, a Witchbane Novella

Dark Rivers

Flame and Ash

Unholy

The Devil You Know

The Christmas Crunch, a Witchbane Short Story

CPSIA information can be obtained
at www.ICGtesting.com
Printed in the USA
LVHW111645270322
714534LV00001B/109